MW00980715

THIS WAY TO HEAVEN

Jasmina laughed loudly as she struggled to control Lightning as he skittered across the path, tossing his head and chomping on his bit.

Lightning was certainly a marvellous ride, fast and strong.

Then the stupid stallion had spooked when a small rabbit ran across his path.

Just as she had been about to get Lightning under control, a great black and silver car came roaring round the bend and it took all her skill as a rider to stop her mount from bolting.

She was still struggling to quieten him when a man jumped out of the car, shouting at her, his face dark with anger and grabbed hold of the bridle.

"*You little fool!* Who on earth put you up on such a powerful animal? Get down at once!"

Jasmina gathered the reins tightly in her hands and tugged the bridle away from the dark-haired stranger who was glaring up at her in a passion of fury.

"Please stop shouting at me! You are only making the horse more anxious."

"Why, you're an American!"

THE BARBARA CARTLAND PINK COLLECTION

Titles in this series

THIS WAY TO HEAVEN

BARBARA CARTLAND

Barbaracartland.com Ltd

© 2008 by Cartland Promotions
First published on the internet in November 2008
by Barbaracartland.com

ISBN 978-1-905155-98-9

*The characters and situations in this book are entirely
imaginary and bear no relation to any real person or
actual happening.*

This book is sold subject to the condition that it shall not,
by way of trade or otherwise, be lent, resold, hired out or
otherwise circulated without the publisher's prior consent.

No part of this publication may be reproduced or
transmitted in any form or by any means, electronically or
mechanically, including photocopying, recording or any
information storage or retrieval, without the prior
permission in writing from the publisher.

Printed and bound in Great Britain by Cle-Print Ltd.
of St Ives, Cambridgeshire.

THE BARBARA CARTLAND PINK COLLECTION

Barbara Cartland was the most prolific bestselling author in the history of the world. She was frequently in the Guinness Book of Records for writing more books in a year than any other living author. In fact her most amazing literary feat was when her publishers asked for more Barbara Cartland romances, she doubled her output from 10 books a year to over 20 books a year, when she was 77.

She went on writing continuously at this rate for 20 years and wrote her last book at the age of 97, thus completing 400 books between the ages of 77 and 97.

Her publishers finally could not keep up with this phenomenal output, so at her death she left 160 unpublished manuscripts, something again that no other author has ever achieved.

Now the exciting news is that these 160 original unpublished Barbara Cartland books are already being published and by Barbaracartland.com exclusively on the internet, as the international web is the best possible way of reaching so many Barbara Cartland readers around the world.

The 160 books are published monthly and will be numbered in sequence.

The series is called the Pink Collection as a tribute to Barbara Cartland whose favourite colour was pink and it became very much her trademark over the years.

The Barbara Cartland Pink Collection is published only on the internet. Log on to www.barbaracartland.com to find out how you can purchase the books monthly as they are published, and take out a subscription that will ensure that all subsequent editions are delivered to you by mail order to your home.

NEW

Barbaracartland.com is proud to announce the publication of ten new Audio Books for the first time as CDs. They are favourite Barbara Cartland stories read by well-known actors and actresses and each story extends to 4 or 5 CDs. The Audio Books are as follows :

The Patient Bridegroom	The Passion and the Flower
A Challenge of Hearts	Little White Doves of Love
A Train to Love	The Prince and the Pekinese
The Unbroken Dream	A King in Love
The Cruel Count	A Sign of Love

More Audio Books will be published in the future and the above titles can be purchased by logging on to the website www.barbaracartland.com or please write to the address below.

If you do not have access to a computer, you can write for information about the Barbara Cartland Pink Collection and the Barbara Cartland Audio Books to the following address:

Barbara Cartland.com Ltd., Camfield Place,
Hatfield, Hertfordshire AL9 6JE, United Kingdom.
Telephone: +44 (0)1707 642629
Fax: +44 (0)1707 663041

THE LATE DAME BARBARA CARTLAND

Barbara Cartland who sadly died in May 2000 at the age of nearly 99 was the world's most famous romantic novelist who wrote 723 books in her lifetime with worldwide sales of over 1 billion copies and her books were translated into 36 different languages.

As well as romantic novels, she wrote historical biographies, 6 autobiographies, theatrical plays, books of advice on life, love, vitamins and cookery. She also found time to be a political speaker and television and radio personality.

She wrote her first book at the age of 21 and this was called *Jigsaw*. It became an immediate bestseller and sold 100,000 copies in hardback and was translated into 6 different languages. She wrote continuously throughout her life, writing bestsellers for an astonishing 76 years. Her books have always been immensely popular in the United States, where in 1976 her current books were at numbers 1 & 2 in the B. Dalton bestsellers list, a feat never achieved before or since by any author.

Barbara Cartland became a legend in her own lifetime and will be best remembered for her wonderful romantic novels, so loved by her millions of readers throughout the world.

Her books will always be treasured for their moral message, her pure and innocent heroines, her good looking and dashing heroes and above all her belief that the power of love is more important than anything else in everyone's life.

"We all seek Heaven and some of us are lucky enough to find it, but the only way to reach Heaven is through Love, which is the closest man can ever get to God."

Barbara Cartland

CHAPTER ONE
1908

"Oh dear, Jasmina, I do feel so dreadful, leaving you in such a fashion!"

Margaret, the Duchess of Harley, stood at the top of the long flight of stone steps that led from the great door of Harley Court down to the wide gravel driveway that circled a vast ornate fountain.

A brisk November wind was tearing the remaining yellow and bronze leaves from the avenue of fine oaks that bordered the drive all the way towards the great ornamental gates at the far end.

Beyond the gates was the road that led through the woods and up into the hills towards the pass through to the town of Debbingford in the next valley.

In the other direction, the hills rose up one after the other until they reached the wild heather covered Yorkshire moors.

The Duchess was a short plump lady and she was wrapped in layers of heavy winter clothes and wearing a huge hat tied under her chin with a silk scarf.

To an onlooker she appeared almost a comical little figure, looking almost as wide as she was tall.

Now she gazed up at the tall slender American girl standing next to her with a worried expression on her kind face.

"Are you sure you would not be better coming with me to London?"

Jasmina Winfield smiled down at her distant cousin with real affection.

"Now, Aunt Margaret, we have discussed this many times. You are greatly needed in London and as I have already seen something of that wonderful City, I am to go to my mother's cousins at the Parsonage in Debbingford for a few weeks and experience a real English Christmas."

The Duchess clutched at her long floating scarf that was in danger of being blown away. She wrapped it firmly round her neck and wished, not for the first time that day that Albert, her husband the Duke, was not so far away on business in Scotland.

Their only daughter, Hope, was married to the Earl of Leyton and news had arrived the night before to Harley Grange that the infant heir to the Earldom had been born into this world three weeks early.

The Duchess was desperate to travel to London to be at her daughter's bedside.

But she had a houseguest – an American relation, Jasmina Winfield, but what was to become of her?

They had only been at home in Yorkshire for three days after a few weeks at their London house.

Jasmina knew no one in the area and there had been no time for introductions.

She sighed.

The Duchess had been hesitating on the steps for a good ten minutes now and she could see that the chauffeur was growing restless.

The luggage had been loaded into the Rolls Royce and her cousin's maid was standing shivering by the side of the car.

"Aunt Margaret," declared Jasmina firmly, placing a gentle hand under her arm and escorting her slowly down the stone steps. "It is much too cold a day for you to stand outside. If you catch a chill, you will not be able to help Hope with her darling little boy."

"Oh dear, oh dear, yes, well, if you are quite sure. Now, do be very careful on your journey when you leave, Jasmina. The roads are so treacherous at this time of year."

Jasmina smiled.

She was from a part of America – Missouri, where the winters were always terribly hard. She was very used to low temperatures and thick snowfalls.

By comparison Northern England in the month of November had seemed very tame.

"I shall be most careful, do not fear. Now, off you go, Aunt Margaret. Give my love to Hope and write to me at my cousin's address with all the news."

The Duchess hesitated a few seconds longer. She was still feeling uneasy.

This young American cousin was so different from the English girls of her age.

Jasmina was extremely independent and held some determined views. She had shocked some of the Duchess's elderly friends with her outspoken comments about politics and how to cure poverty in the most destitute areas of big cities.

The Duchess sighed loudly as she took her seat in the Rolls. She was more than certain that America was a fine place, but it did seem to breed a very headstrong type of young woman!

At long last the car drove away down the drive, the Duchess waving her handkerchief from the window until it passed out of sight.

Jasmina looked relieved.

She was extremely fond of the lady she called Aunt Margaret, although she was not her aunt, of course, but a distant cousin on her father's side.

Jasmina was born and bred in America, but all her life she had longed to visit England. She had read every book and travel guide she could find and asked her long-suffering parents many questions about their family in that distant country.

At long last, when she reached the age of twenty-one, her father had given in to her pestering and arranged for her to cross the Atlantic to stay with his relations, the Duke and Duchess of Harley and their family.

To Jasmina, tall and fair, with sparkling blue eyes and a determined expression, London had been everything she had ever imagined.

She had enjoyed the shops, the ancient buildings, the parties and balls. She had loved visiting the historical places she had only read about, learning the manners and traditions of a different world.

But it was not until she travelled up to the family's ancestral home in Yorkshire on the edge of the moors that she felt her spirits lift with unexpected joy.

Jasmina had never seen such beautiful countryside and she knew with all her soul that even when she returned home, part of her heart would stay here.

Now she ran nimbly up the stone steps and into the huge echoing hall with its superb black and white marble floor and graceful Grecian statues brought back to England by one of the Duke's ancestors.

She would be very sad to leave Harley Grange, but was sensible enough to know it would be inadvisable to stay there on her own.

Back home in Missouri, she would not have given it another thought. But even though they were now in a new century, Jasmina was aware that many of her family's acquaintances still adhered to the old ways of manners and decorum.

So she would depart for the Parsonage, to the other cousins who lived in the village of Debbingford twenty miles away in the next valley.

She had assured Aunt Margaret that she would be perfectly safe travelling there on her own.

Goodness, at home in Missouri, most friends lived more than twenty miles away and you often went to their houses just for lunch or an afternoon visit!

"Miss Winfield – "

It was Reid, the elderly butler.

"Yes, Reid. Can I help you?"

"Just to inform you, miss, that the horse His Grace purchased recently has just arrived. It has been stabled and cared for, but I thought it best that you knew."

"Oh, yes, Reid. Thank you! The Duke told me in London before he left for Scotland that this is the mount he wanted me to ride while I was here at Harley Grange.

"It is vastly annoying that the dealer has delayed in sending the animal. I am so looking forward to seeing him. I must go down to the stables. Perhaps I could take him out for just a short ride before I leave."

Reid's mouth tightened.

This young American lady was certainly pleasant, but surely she should know that it was not suitable for her to ride around the countryside on a strange horse. Well, maybe in America things were handled differently, but this was Harley Grange in England.

"Maybe it would not be advisable, Miss Winfield. The Head Groom is away on estate business and I believe the animal is extremely highly strung."

Jasmina was about to inform the butler that she had been riding since she was three and could handle any horse given her.

But she hesitated, as she was well aware that there were differences in the way Society worked over here in England and although it was irritating, well, there was no reason to antagonise the staff.

No, what the eye did not see, the heart would not grieve over – that was what her old Nanny would have said and at the moment Jasmina thought this was very good advice.

She ran up to her room and began to sort out the clothes she would need for the following day.

Because she had just had the most marvellous idea – a wonderful plan.

She would ride the new horse across country to her cousins in Debbingford!

She knew these cousins were not as wealthy as the Duke and Duchess and so she was not sure if they would have a mount for her. It seemed such a shame to leave the animal in the stables when he had been purchased just for her.

The casement window now rattled violently and she hurried across to close it.

Gazing out, she could see, on a far distant hill, the brooding turreted outline of Somerton Castle.

Jasmina realised that the immense Somerton estate bordered on the Duke's land and was intrigued by the story the Duchess had told her over supper the night before.

"Oh, my dear, it is so sad. Richard, the present Earl of Somerton, is a tragic figure. A real recluse. He sees no one!"

Jasmina had gazed at the Duchess across the candle flames, her sapphire eyes sparkling.

"No one at all? My word, what would he do if you called?"

"I would be told firmly that he is not at home. My dear Albert meets him occasionally on estate business and I believe he undertakes various work for the Government so he does travel down to London. But, apart from that, he never appears in Society."

"But why? Is he perhaps – " Jasmina hesitated, searching for the right words, "disfigured in some way?"

"Oh, no, my dear, Richard was always the best-looking young man and even now at thirty he is most distinguished. But – " she leant dramatically across the table – "he lost Millicent, his wife, two years ago. A tragic accident. Dreadful. She was so young, so pretty. He has never been the same since."

Now from her bedroom window, Jasmina gazed out at the distant castle.

She would have loved to have met the Earl.

He sounded such a romantic, tragic figure. Like a character in a novel.

But now she was leaving the district, even though temporarily, there would be no immediate opportunity for their paths to cross."

*

The next day dawned cold and dull and the sullen sky hung grey over the Yorkshire countryside, threatening snow later in the day.

Richard, the Earl of Somerton, sat drinking coffee in the dismal breakfast room of Somerton Castle.

He had told his staff not to bother lighting the fire this morning, because he was going to be away from home in London for a few days.

But now he shivered in the chilly room.

"More coffee, my Lord?"

His housekeeper, Mary Landrey was at his shoulder.

"No, thank you, Mary. And you can clear away the food as well."

She bit her lip as she could see that he had eaten nothing. The hot dishes of crispy bacon, succulent local sausages and scrambled egg remained untouched.

"Shall I ask cook for more toast, my Lord? We do have some new plum preserve and – "

"Nothing, thank you, Mary. I shall be leaving for London within minutes. But do make sure this food does not go to waste. I am sure the staff will enjoy it."

She bent her head in exasperated acknowledgement and signalled to Gladys, the maid, to clear away.

The breakfast would all go to waste. The servants would be appalled to be offered cold eggs and bacon!

Mary watched from the door as the Earl stirred his coffee.

She could tell he was in one of his black moods, those great bouts of depression that came down on him like thunder clouds.

She sighed and twisted her hands together under her white starched apron.

She had wanted to speak to her Master today about George Radford, but this was obviously not a good time.

Mary was slim, dark-haired with worried grey eyes. At twenty-five, she was rather young for her position as housekeeper to a great castle and family, but in reality her job was very simple as the Earl no longer entertained or had visitors.

It had all been so different some years ago, when she had been appointed lady's maid to Millicent, the late Lady Somerton.

Millicent had only been thirteen when her parents died in a tragic boating accident on the River Thames in

London and she had been left as ward to the then Earl of Somerton.

People had felt pity for a young girl going to live with such a brusque military man, but as it turned out, he had doted on the child, giving her everything she desired and never saying no to whatever fancy she asked for.

Then, three years ago, when Millicent was sixteen, the old Earl had died and his son Richard, who had been away in India in the Army, had inherited the title.

On his return to England, he had married the young Millicent and Mary had been promoted from parlour-maid to lady's maid.

It was difficult, looking at the Earl's serious dark eyes and frowning expression to recall those happier days. There had been parties, dinners, dancing and music.

Privately Mary had never reckoned the Earl to be deeply in love with his young wife, but, like his father before him, he had indulged her every whim and that some whispered, had cost her life.

And when pretty silly Lady Somerton died in that dreadful accident, the Earl had shut up most of the castle and shunned the world.

Mary had thought she would be out of a job, but to her great surprise, the Earl had offered her the position of housekeeper.

Why had she accepted his offer? Life at the castle was bleakly quiet these days.

The Earl had a very uncertain temper and the black moods that descended on him made him a difficult employer.

But if she was honest, she knew why.

Mary had given her heart to a young local farmer, George Radford, and although he told her he could not afford to marry her, she knew she would never willingly move from Somerton to a place where she might never see George again.

"I shall be away for two or three days in London, Mary," the Earl now said, standing up abruptly. "You can, of course, reach me at the Knightsbridge house if there are any emergencies."

"Yes, my Lord. Shall I ask Mills to bring the car round at once?"

"Yes, please do so. I have told Fergus he need not accompany me and tell Mills I will drive myself."

Mary sighed.

It seemed that the Earl no longer even wished for the company of his valet or chauffeur when he travelled to London.

He was withdrawing himself more and more from the world. It was exceedingly worrying, but there was no one she could talk to about the problem.

She made her way back along the stone passage, through the baize door that led to the kitchen and told Mills to bring the car to the castle courtyard.

Mrs. Rush, the cook, gave her a sharpish look and poured her out a large mug of tea.

"Driving himself again, is he?"

Mary nodded.

"Not even taking Fergus with him."

Mrs. Rush pursed her lips in annoyance and pushed down the sleeves of the black dress she wore under her voluminous white apron.

She was a stout jolly Yorkshire woman with a mop of grey curls she kept bundled up under a big, white, frilly cap. Her round face was red with the heat from the stove.

"It b'aint right, the Lord goin' to London without any servants to attend him. What will the Knightsbridge staff think of us? They'll reckon we're no better than poor savages who know no better how to behave!"

"I know, Mrs. Rush, but what can we do? He even told Fergus to tell the Reverend Parker he was not at home when the vicar called! And Doctor Meade was very put out when he rode over from Debbingford just to call on his Lordship and was told he could not be seen."

"From what young Gladys brought downstairs, his Lordship has only had one cup of coffee this mornin' and no breakfast at all. Not even a small spoonful of my lovely porridge. And him travellin' all the way to London!"

She banged down the mixing bowl she was holding on the table and began to pummel the dough inside it.

"It b'aint right, Mary. I'd hoped he would begin to come out of his grief this year, but he seems to be getting' worse. All callers are turned away, even the Duchess of Harley was told he was not at home!

"And there's to be no Christmas party for the staff, I hear. And no Christmas tree! That's shameful, so it is!"

The dough was given another fierce pummelling.

"I blame that silly girl gettin' herself killed!"

"Mrs. Rush! You must not speak ill of the dead. She was my Lady and a nice little thing, even if she was a scatterbrain."

Cook sniffed disdainfully. She had been in service at the castle since the Earl was a baby. All her loyalty lay with him.

And, like most of the old family retainers, she was well aware that there was no direct heir at the moment.

If anything, God forbid, should happen to the Earl, then the title would pass to a very distant cousin who kept sheep out in Australia.

She glanced at Mary's drawn and worried face.

11

"Did you get a chance to mention that there George Radford to his Lordship?"

Mary shook her head.

"It didn't seem to be the right time. Oh, Mrs. Rush, if only George would sell his little plot of land to the Earl! It's not large enough to support a family and the Earl has offered George a good sum for it, especially as it separates those two big woods he's so fond of riding in. If George had the money, we could afford to get married."

"Ah, it's all about his pride with George Radford," cook said darkly. "He says that there piece of damp old ground has been in his family for as long as the Somerton estate has been in theirs!"

Mary nodded and returned to her tea.

The elderly cook was quite right. She loved George Radford with her whole heart, but he just could not see that giving in and selling his land would mean they could buy a little farm somewhere else and get married.

The Earl was just as determined that he should sell. And the bad feeling between the two of them had made her position very difficult.

She shivered, even though the kitchen was warm.

She glanced out of the window at the leaden sky. It would snow soon – having been born and bred in the valley, she recognised the signs.

Mary now wished that she had been brave enough to speak to the Earl this morning. To try and explain that George was not being insolent or rude, just stubborn.

And how she wished that the Earl would meet some nice sensible lady while he was in London and find some happiness again.

Surely then, he would not be so hard to approach with estate problems?

Jasmina woke early, washed and pulled on the long leather riding trousers she had brought with her from her home in America.

She packed some essential toiletries and a change of clothing into her small overnight case, which could be fastened on the back of her saddle. The rest of her luggage could be sent over the following day.

Jasmina was only too aware that her cousins at the Debbingford Parsonage were not very well off.

She was certain there would not be many occasions where she would need a ball dress!

She ran downstairs and called 'good morning' to the three maids who were already hard at work polishing the great wooden staircase.

They bobbed their heads to her as she passed and Jasmina wondered to herself if she would ever get used to the different approach the servants had in England.

Reid appeared as she hurried across the hall and towards the door that led out into the stable yard.

"Will you be taking breakfast, Miss Winfield?"

"Oh, no. Please tell the cook not to bother on my account. I'm sure my cousins will give me a good lunch and I do not like riding when I have just eaten."

Reid appeared startled out of his usual impassive expression.

"Riding, Miss Winfield? I thought you would be taking the carriage – "

"Oh, no," Jasmina remarked airily. "I agreed with the Duchess yesterday that I would ride to Debbingford. I will need a horse and, as you know, the Duke has kindly bought me one."

Reid looked concerned.

"But the weather is about to change, Miss Winfield. It will snow heavily before the day is out."

Jasmina tossed her head, her golden curls dancing as they tried to escape from the heavy leather cap she had pulled over them.

She had no doubt that any snow Yorkshire could produce would be but nothing compared with what she was used to at home.

And what was twenty miles? Just a short trip!

The stable block was already busy in the cold early morning light.

The lads were brushing down the yard, the horses had all been groomed and stood, their heads over the doors of their stalls, watching the yard with interest.

Jasmina approached the new horse with a sense of excitement. She knew his name was Lightning and he was a shiny black with a white star on his proud forehead.

She patted his velvety nose and admired the fine shape of his head.

The young stable lad looked startled when Jasmina asked him to saddle up Lightning.

"But miss – " he began. "We don't know yet what he be like to ride. The groom who delivered him said he had could be mischievous, like."

Jasmina laughed, her beautiful face radiant with her enjoyment of life.

"Please don't worry. I am quite certain I'll be fine. I intend to ride him over to Debbingford this morning and it will give me a good chance to test out all his paces. The Duke told me that there was a fine leather saddle ready for the new horse, so please get him ready immediately."

"But the snow, miss!"

"It hasn't started to fall yet! I will be safely indoors in Debbingford by the time it does."

*

The Earl of Somerton drove out of the castle, down a steep hill and out into the narrow winding lane that led to the main road.

He cast a quick look up at the sky.

He was certain that snow would fall tonight. And a lot of it, if he was not mistaken.

There was indeed a sullen leaden look to the clouds hanging so low above the distant moors that they seemed to be touching them.

The cold bleak day suited the Earl's mood.

He had no desire to travel to London, but equally no desire to stay in Yorkshire for Christmas.

He felt as though he was spending his waking hours existing, finding things to do to keep busy.

He knew his friends wanted him to enter Society once more, but he could not force himself to do so.

All the glittering scene of dances and balls, Ascot, Henley, theatres, none of it seemed real to him any more.

It was as if on that fateful day two years ago, the day his sweet childish Millicent had died, he had slammed a door on the life he had once had and this dark existence was all that was left.

Savagely, his suppressed feelings getting the better of him, he pressed down hard on the car's accelerator and the powerful car roared forward.

Spinning the wheel, he steered around a sharp bend too quickly and then yelled in horror.

A young girl on horseback was in the middle of the road. The animal, a huge black beast, was rearing and at the sight of the car, it tried to bolt.

Even as the Earl stopped the car with a screech of brakes and leapt out, he knew that whoever the rider was, she was handling the animal magnificently.

But those were not the words that came tumbling from his mouth.

"*You little idiot!*" he shouted. "What the heck do you think you are doing? Do you want to get yourself killed?"

And as he strode towards her, his face was dark with anger.

CHAPTER TWO

Jasmina laughed loudly as she struggled to control Lightning as he skittered across the path, tossing his head and chomping on his bit.

She was enjoying her journey to her cousin's home in Debbingford in the next valley. Lightning was certainly a marvellous ride, fast and strong.

The beautiful saddle of fine pale leather the Duke had purchased for her was extremely comfortable, although strange in shape to the American saddles she was used to back home in Missouri.

Then the stupid stallion had spooked when a small rabbit ran across his path.

Just as she had been about to get Lightning under control, a great black and silver car came roaring round the bend and it took all her skill as a rider to stop her mount from bolting.

She was still struggling to quieten him when a man jumped out of the car, shouting at her, his face dark with anger and grabbed hold of the bridle.

"*You little fool*! Who on earth put you up on such a powerful animal? Get down at once!"

Jasmina gathered the reins tightly in her hands and tugged the bridle away from the dark-haired stranger who was glaring up at her in a passion of fury.

"Please stop shouting at me! You are only making the horse more anxious."

"Why, you're an American!"

Jasmina now circled Lightning, her voice calming him until he stood, quivering slightly, but under control – for the moment.

"Yes, sir, I am indeed from the United States where we would consider it a sin to drive so fast on a narrow road where people could well be out riding!"

The Earl frowned.

It was not often that he felt at a disadvantage, but this beautiful, slim, blue-eyed girl was staring down at him from astride the big stallion with an expression on her face that told him she thought he was the one in the wrong.

"Are you going to dismount, madam?"

Jasmina gazed down at her protagonist.

He was tall and broad-shouldered, the cut of his suit telling her that he was a wealthy man, even if the Rolls Royce had failed to do so.

But wealthy or not, his orders, barked out in that rude fashion were most unwelcome.

"Certainly *not*, sir. I am in complete control and I would be grateful if you would stand out of my way, so I can continue my journey."

The Earl's frown darkened even more.

"Madam, there is no way I can possibly allow you to ride off on that animal. He has a malicious expression in his eyes. I have seen it before on rogue horses. You will not be safe."

Jasmina tossed her head in sheer annoyance, bright golden curls escaping from beneath her riding cap.

"I do thank you for your concern, kind sir, but it is misplaced. I have been riding all my life. I know exactly what I am doing and your assistance is not required!"

The Earl felt his temper snap.

The picture flashed into his mind of another strong-willed young girl – one who had tried to jump a fence that was too big for her mount, even though he had begged her not to do so.

Millicent, his poor little wife.

He could still hear her laughing as she attempted to make her horse obey her commands and her cry as she was thrown – to lie, lifeless, on the ground.

Jasmina gasped as the man standing by her stirrup reached up and she saw he was about to pull her from the saddle.

Was he a madman?

She suddenly realised that the road was surrounded by dense woods. It was a lonely and isolated place and no one would see if he attacked her.

But Jasmina was no shrinking violet.

When other girls would have screamed for help, she gritted her teeth and without hesitating, dug her heels into her mount's sides and tightened the reins.

Lightning reared up and whinnied, his black eyes ringed with white and his flashing hooves just missing the man's head.

Then Jasmina had turned him and urged him into a canter away from the man and his car.

Lightning needed no encouragement.

Mud spattered from his hooves as he pounded away down the track into the shelter of the woods.

The Earl swore under his breath as he watched the girl on the big black horse vanish from sight.

He wondered if he should drive after her.

He was sure the horse was a rogue and not safe for anyone to ride. He could see that the American girl was a good equestrienne, but would that be enough to keep her from harm?

He shivered as a gust of freezing wind blew in from the hills above his castle and gazed up into a sky that was heavy and sullen with snow clouds before striding back to the Rolls Royce.

If he could not reach the main road in the next ten minutes, he knew the pass over the moors would be closed, probably for days and the valley would be cut off from the outside world.

He understood this winter weather only too well. Once it came in from the North and East, the snow settled on the hard Yorkshire ground and drifted in the wind.

Part of him knew that he should follow the girl and make sure she was safe, but, as he glanced at the slim black briefcase on the seat next to him, he realised that he must take these important papers to London. They were vital for the talks that were to take place in Whitehall in the New Year.

'Well, no doubt Miss America is nearly home by now – wherever home might be, or tipped into a ditch!' he muttered to himself.

He started the engine and drove away, refusing to admit how startling and unsettling the incident had made him feel.

Memories of Millicent and her tragic accident came crowding in onto him yet again and the sparkle that his encounter with the blonde rider had brought back to his eyes now vanished as he felt the weight of a familiar black depression settle on his shoulders.

*

Jasmina slowed Lightning to a walk, glancing back over her shoulder to make quite certain that the dark-eyed stranger had not followed her in his car.

What a very odd man!

The passion and anger in his voice and on his face had left her strangely disturbed.

She could still see those piercing dark eyes gazing up at her. Admittedly they had looked angry, but they had also held an expression of great sadness.

'I declare I expect he has some poor wife at home, who has always had to put up with that bad temper of his,' she conjectured. 'I pity her with all my heart. I for one could never marry a man with such a bad nature!'

Jasmina tossed her head again.

She had most decided views about who she would marry one day.

She knew she would only link her life with a man for love because it would have to be forever.

She had known too many friends who had travelled to England with their inheritance in order to marry some impoverished Duke or Earl and help rebuild his rundown estate.

Well, that certainly was not going to happen to her. '*No way*,' as Jeremy, her old groom would say back home.

Fancy being faced with that bad-tempered man and being told he was your future husband!

She could feel her heart beating faster than usual and her forehead was hot even though the temperature had fallen dramatically in the last few minutes.

Jasmina gazed up at the sky, just as the wind began to sweep icily down the track from the hills and the first fat flakes of snow began to fall.

'Oh jeez, the weather's changing, just as Reid said it would. We had better hurry up, Lightning. We need to get to the Parsonage at Debbingford and *fast*!'

She came to a fork in the track and hesitated.

The signpost said she should ride straight on, but surely if she cut downwards into the valley, she could ride round the lake she could see and then straight up the hill to the pass.

That would save a good five miles and she would be in Debbingford inside twenty minutes.

The wind whistled shrilly as she turned Lightning off the beaten path, but she ignored all her misgivings.

She was from Missouri and she was used to riding in bad weather.

There was no chance she was going to meekly trot home and confess to the staff of Harley Grange that she was not as strong and resourceful as an English girl!

She pulled a waterproof cape from her saddlebag and slid it over her head. It would help keep her dry.

Urging Lightning into a fast walk, Jasmina did not look back and therefore failed to see that her wallet with her passport, money and all the letters of introduction the Duchess had given her, had been pulled out of her bag with the cape and now lay at the side of the road, being swiftly buried under inches of snow.

*

George Radford trudged wearily through the snow, leading his stocky little grey pony.

The blizzard howled bleakly through the trees and every now and then he could hear an ominous crack as yet another branch finally gave up its fight against the weight of snow.

George pulled his collar tight round his mouth and chin.

He had been lucky to get out of Debbingford when he did.

A few minutes later and the only pass over the hills would have been closed.

22

As it was, it had been difficult and his trousers were soaked up to his knees where he had struggled through a deep drift.

He plodded on slowly with a heavy heart, hardly able to feel his feet and fingers.

Getting up before dawn, travelling all that way into the next valley and what for? Just to sell a few eggs and parsnips!

The money he had taken had gone straight into the pockets of the corn merchants for next year's seed! Well, Christmas would indeed be a gloomy affair this year.

'And Mary reckons I could afford to marry 'er and keep a home!' he muttered. 'If the Earl would only sell me another couple of acres, I might well do so, but he's like all the aristocracy. They hang on to every inch of their land, whether they need it or not.'

George felt the familiar anger building up inside him. The Earl wanted him to sell the plot of land that had been in his family for so long and then two parts of his estate could be connected.

But that piece of land had belonged to the Radfords for centuries.

No Somerton had ever asked to buy it before and George was determined he would never sell it.

His old Dad would surely turn in his grave at the very thought.

Now he peered into the swirling blizzard to check where he was. Even with the path under a foot of snow, these woods were an open book to him.

There was the old dead oak tree and the great holly bush right next to it, the berries gleaming scarlet through the white covering.

'I reckon my Mary would like a bit of 'olly for the

castle,' George muttered to his pony. 'Won't take me a minute to cut 'er a bit. She can 'ang it in the servants' hall if the Earl won't 'ave it in the main rooms.'

He tethered his mount in the shelter of a thick bush and then strode off the path.

Suddenly he cursed and stumbled.

"What the blazes?"

He knelt down and scraped away at a covering of snow.

To his astonishment, a dark waterproof cape came into his view and, as he pulled it back, the pale face of a beautiful young girl appeared, her skin almost as white as the snow flakes gently settling on her lips and eyelashes.

*

Mary and Mrs. Rush were alone in the vast castle kitchen, sipping their afternoon tea.

It was so dark outside that they had already lit the oil lamps that were now shining down onto the scrubbed wooden counter tops, as the copper pans reflected back the light and on the great dark oak dressers, the blue and white kitchen china added a flash of colour.

Most of the staff had been given the afternoon off, but because of the weather were sitting in the servants' hall down the corridor, gossiping.

Pardew, the butler, had taken his cup of tea and a buttered scone and retired to his pantry, where he cleaned the family silver.

Mary wondered if he might be slipping the odd tot of whisky into his tea. She had sometimes smelt it on his breath and he went to bed extremely early these days.

She sighed.

In a well-run establishment, she would have been able to tackle Pardew and point out that his behaviour was not acceptable, but she knew he was bored because there was nothing to do here at the castle.

The Earl no longer invited the local gentry to dinner parties or entertained in any fashion at all. Since his wife's death, he had retired completely from Society and it made life for his butler extremely tame.

And if Mary were to speak to the Earl, what would happen?

Like as not he would not back her action.

He did not care what happened below stairs. Not as long as he was not bothered and not forced out of his deep dark depression.

Mary sighed again as she stared out of the window at the swirling snow.

She knew only too well what a blizzard like this meant.

The castle would be cut off for days, all the roads leading to it would become impassable and even when they cleared, the routes into the local towns would still be shut.

"At least there's no need to worry about what to serve our guests for Christmas," she moaned to Mrs. Rush. "Seeing as we won't be having any!"

Mrs. Rush tutted and sipped her tea.

"I've made some lovely Christmas puddings, just as usual, but I can't see the Master eating any festive fare."

Mary stood up, smoothing down her dark dress and checking that the important household keys were hanging safely from her leather belt.

Regardless of the empty castle, she would do her rounds of the four turrets and all the rooms and corridors that linked them.

With the Earl so distant from his staff, it was easy for the younger maids to fall into bad habits.

Sometimes Mary would find staircases that had not been swept or rooms where the drapes had not been dusted for weeks or the windows opened to prevent damp.

She was more than conscious that she was so very young for such a responsible job and was determined not to disappoint the Earl in any way.

A violent knocking at the scullery door made her jump.

"Who on earth is that, out in this weather?" said Mrs. Rush.

Mary ran into the scullery to unlatch the back door and had to fight to open it against the howling gale as the banging sounded again.

To her astonishment George, the man she loved so much, staggered indoors carrying a large burden covered in snow.

He gasped for breath as the warmth of the kitchen caught in his throat.

"George! Whatever's happened?"

"Here! Quick! It's a young lady. Found her out in Bridgend Woods. Can't tell if she's alive or dead!"

"*What*? Oh, my goodness! Mrs. Rush! Quickly, please bring towels and stoke up the fire. And we'll need blankets and brandy too. Bring her over here, George, and lay her down alongside the fire. Where did you say you found her?"

"Over in Bridgend Woods. She's a-wearing ridin' clothes and right strange ones at that, but there was no sign of any 'orse. I reckon she was thrown. Look – see that cut and bump on her forehead? She was lyin' beside a big old tree trunk. That's what I reckon she hit her 'ead on when she fell."

Mary smoothed the soaking wet hair back from the girl's brow.

She slid her finger to one side of her throat and frowned.

Was there a pulse?

"Yes! She's alive! Thank God for that! Listen, we must call the doctor and hope he can take her away to a hospital immediately."

She glanced up at George and felt the colour rising in her cheeks at the warmth of his gaze.

Then she realised the young farmer was shaking his head, the snowflakes melting on his dark red hair.

"No, Mary. The nearest doctor is Doctor Meade in Debbingford and there's no way that he can get 'ere. The snow's already several feet deep. The castle's cut off from the town."

Mrs. Rush hurried into the room and helped Mary pull the waterproof cape from the girl's still body.

"We need to get her out of these wet clothes and into a warm bed or she won't stay alive for long!"

Mary bit her lip.

"But we can't possibly keep her in the castle, Mrs. Rush! The Earl would never allow it. Heavens, he refuses to even see callers, people he's known all his life, let alone have a strange invalid staying here for goodness knows how long!"

The elderly cook pursed her lips and chaffed at the girl's hands.

"What the eyes don't see, the heart won't grieve over."

Mary stared at her for a second and then made up her mind.

"George – you must carry her upstairs. We can't deal with her on the kitchen floor! Mrs. Rush, bring the hot water and brandy."

George picked up the girl as if she weighed nothing and followed Mary out of the kitchen and down the long staff corridor.

Their feet were very silent on the rough matting and then they ascended the cold winding stone steps the maids climbed to reach the top floors of the castle without using the main staircase.

Mary now picked up an oil lamp and hurried along a narrow corridor to a room in the south turret of the castle.

"Quick! In here. Put her down on the bed – gently now, George. The poor thing. I wonder who she is? She certainly isn't anyone who lives locally."

"Well, reckon we just won't know until she comes round – if she ever does!" said George gloomily.

He backed right away from the bed, glancing round nervously at the fine curtains and thick rugs on the floor.

"Whose room is this, then, Mary? It's all made up ready. Is the Earl expecting guests for Christmas?"

Mary was about to answer when Mrs. Rush hurried in with a large bowl of hot water and George hastily left the room as the women began to strip off the girl's soaking wet clothes.

"Why put her in this room?" Mrs. Rush enquired, anxiously. "It hasn't been used since – "

"It's the only one with the bed made up and furthest away from the North Turret and his Lordship's room."

"You'll lose your place here if he ever finds out!"

Mary hesitated for just a second and then shrugged as they wrapped the warm towels around the girl.

A small moan escaped her lips – that was indeed marvellous! It proved she was still alive.

"Shall I fetch one of my nightgowns?" asked Mrs. Rush. "Although it would go round her several times, I'm thinking!"

Mary blotted the girl's hair again with a thin linen towel. Under her hands the water was vanishing and a riot of blonde curls was appearing.

"No – wait – in that dresser, Mrs. Rush. Yes, that big one over there in the corner. In the top drawer, you'll find a nightgown."

Mrs. Rush looked startled, but obediently pulled a fine white silk nightdress from the drawer. It was beautiful with exquisite lace frills sewn at the neck and cuffs of the long sleeves.

The cook fingered the soft material before looking across questioningly at the housekeeper, her face creased and worried.

"Mary! Surely this is – "

"Yes, it belonged to the Mistress. But there is no one here to worry about that now. This poor girl needs it."

Once the stranger was warm and dry, she lay on the pillows and the two women stood back and stared down at her.

"She looks like one of those angels you see in some of them art books the Master keeps down in his library," whispered Mrs. Rush. "Do you reckon she'll recover?"

Mary put out a hand to feel the girl's forehead. The cut was close to her hairline and hardly noticeable now, but there was a dark bruise forming.

"She's very hot. I do hope she hasn't taken a chill, but Heavens knows it will be a real miracle if she has come through all this unscathed."

"She seems to be sleepin'."

Mary nodded.

"Yes, and that's a good thing. Hopefully she will waken in the morning with only a bad headache to remind her of her adventure."

"And then she can tell us just who she is," the cook said, busily tidying the towels and basin away. "How she got into Bridgend Woods is anyone's guess. There must be her people out there worried sick that she hasn't returned home. And with Christmas nearly on us, too."

"I'll sit with her," said Mary quietly. "Tell George, if he's still here, that I'll try and speak to him tomorrow."

Mrs. Rush sniffed.

"He'll be lucky to get back to his farm through the snow tonight. Reckon he'll bed down in the stables. Still, that'll be warmer than that damp old farm house of his!"

Mary did not reply. Cook knew how she felt about George Radford. Talking did not help. She loved him so much and would have been proud to be his wife.

But George just refused to marry her. He was as stubborn as his old Dad had been. Completely stuck in the past, refusing to move with the times.

She turned down the oil lamp to a small glimmer and sat quietly by the side of the bed.

The minutes ticked past and the girl was breathing a little easier now, but her forehead still felt very hot.

Suddenly as Mary was applying a cool strip of linen soaked in lavender water to her patient's head, there came the sound of a commotion and dogs barking downstairs in the Great Hall.

She spun round and pulled the bedroom door open.

That voice, calling for Mr. Pardew!

It was the Earl.

He had come back. Obviously he had not been able to get through the pass to the main road.

Mary closed the door and turned back towards the bed, feeling sick with worry and apprehension.

Then she gasped.

Two very blue eyes were open and staring up at her from the pale face on the lace pillow.

A hand lifted from the coverlet towards her.

"Where – am – I?" the girl whispered, but as Mary was about to answer her, she heard the Earl calling out,

"Mary! Mary!"

And she knew she must go to him immediately.

CHAPTER THREE

Mary down bent over the bed and put her finger to her lips as the girl was about to speak.

"Hush!" she cautioned. "Do not say a word. You must stay silent. I will be back in an instant."

And she hurried out.

Jasmina lay very still.

She felt most dreadfully hot, her head ached and the room was spinning around her in a most alarming fashion.

What had happened? Where was she now? Back at Harley Grange?

No – the woman who had placed the cool bandage on her forehead was not someone she had ever met before.

And this strange bedroom with its lace trimmings and its beautiful turquoise and gold curtains, embroidered with wonderful peacock tails was certainly not the one she had used in her aunt's home.

Jasmina struggled to sit up and groaned as a flash of pain shot through her head. She sank back again, but her memory was returning.

She had had an accident – but how?

Her horse! Lightning – the snow – had he fallen in a drift?

All she could recall was galloping wildly through the blizzard – then – nothing.

'Oh, my goodness! I reckon I am lucky to be alive. I wonder what happened to Lightning. Oh, I do hope he is not hurt. But who found me and why did they bring me here? Where is here and why did that woman want me to be quiet?'

Once more she tried to get out of bed, but her head was spinning and she knew she would faint if she stood up.

*

Downstairs in the great castle, the Earl crossed to the velvet bell pull by the fireplace in his study and tugged at it in irritation.

He had tried calling for Pardew when he had found the main castle door unlocked on his return home, but there had been no reply.

He was cold, tired and hungry.

He knew that he had not been expected, as he had told his housekeeper that he would be away in London for several days, but surely some members of his staff were on duty?

There was suddenly a gentle knock on the door and Mary hurried in.

Some of the Earl's temper vanished at the sight of her calm face.

He had always liked the girl who had served as his wife's personal lady's maid.

Her smooth dark hair was neatly plaited, arranged round her ears in two thick coils. The white collar of her black dress was as pristine as ever and the keys at her waist jingled in a familiar manner.

"Ah, Mary. As you can see, I am back home again. Where's Pardew? He should still be about, surely. I need a hot drink and something to eat – some soup, cold beef and pickles, perhaps? See what cook can provide."

Mary nodded, trying to keep her breathing steady.

She had run all the way from the South Turret and her heart was racing. She was certain that the Earl could see it beating under her thin black dress.

"I believe Mr. Pardew has retired by now, my Lord. He felt – I think he felt unwell."

It was impossible for her to inform the Earl that his butler had poured half a bottle of the castle's best brandy into his tea and was, even now lying fast asleep, snoring in his pantry!

The Earl looked up sharply from some documents he was studying. He had a very good idea what ailed his butler and knew he had to do something about it very soon. But now was not the time.

He was well aware in his heart of hearts that he was neglecting his servants and that he was not living up to the responsibilities of his position, but somehow he could not summon up the energy to tackle the problem.

"Did the snow prevent you from travelling down to London, my Lord?" Mary asked as she banked up the fire.

"Yes, the pass is closed. No one is getting in or out of the valley for days, perhaps weeks! It is still snowing, harder than ever!"

Mary hesitated.

What on earth was she now supposed to do about the poor girl lying in bed upstairs? How would she be able to return to her own home?

Gathering up her courage, she was about to speak out and confess what had happened, when the Earl said,

"That will be all for now, Mary. The food and the drink, if you please."

Mary returned to the kitchen and gave the order to Mrs. Rush.

"Does he know about old Pardew?" the cook asked as she took a side of beef from the larder and began to cut slices and place them on a plate.

"I have no idea. He used to be concerned about all

the servants, but since my Lady died, he does not seem interested."

Mrs. Rush sniffed.

"That is so true! A drunken butler, no entertainin', not even receivin' any calls from the local gentry and no Christmas party for the castle staff this year! Bless me, I have never heard of such a thing in a well-run house!"

She paused briefly from her tirade before asking,

"Mary, what are you goin' to do about the young lass upstairs?"

George was sitting at the kitchen table, eating a late supper of bread and cheese.

He had looked out at the falling snow and knew it would be very dangerous to try and return to his farm until the morning when the drifts would be easier to see.

Mary hushed her, glancing round to make sure none of the other servants were in the kitchen.

"Hopefully she will be recovered enough to travel by tomorrow. Once she tells us where she is from, perhaps you could help her home, George. Or if she is still cut off by the blizzard, take her to *The Golden Lion* in the village. One thing is certain, she cannot stay here now the Master is home."

"Once his Lordship's supper has been served, I will go and sit with her," offered Mrs. Rush. "You look worn out, young Mary.

"Sit and talk to George here and try and make him see some sense about sellin' his old farm to our Master. Hopefully this young lady will be able to tell me who she is and we can then get this whole problem sorted out before tomorrow."

Mary nodded her thanks.

She was always very grateful for any chance to be in George's company, but realised that nothing she could say would push him into changing his mind about selling his farm.

Those few damp acres had taken on a whole new significance to the young Yorkshireman since the Earl had asked him to sell them to him.

Somehow it was no longer about the land, but two men from different walks of life trying to best each other.

As Mary and George talked in the kitchen, the Earl absentmindedly nodded his thanks when Gladys brought in his supper on a silver tray.

The beef looked fresh and succulent and the bread and pickles wholesome, but he found his appetite had gone.

Moodily he drank the coffee and then pushed the rest aside.

He sat for an hour, staring into the dying embers of the fire.

He knew he should be concentrating on what to do with these vital papers that now were not going to arrive in London in time for the meeting at the Foreign Office.

But instead, all he was able to think about was that impudent American girl riding a black horse that was far too strong for even a good rider such as herself.

He could still see in his mind's eye her sparkling blue eyes as she gazed down at him from her saddle.

Had she reached her destination safely before the blizzard closed all the roads in the district?

He hoped so.

Perhaps he should ask someone – the doctor or the Rector, perhaps, who might possibly have heard about an American houseguest staying locally.

After all, she was a visitor to his country. It would only be courteous to check that she was safe and sound.

He picked up the telephone receiver, then realised

that the line was dead. Of course! He should have guessed that the snow would cut off all communication.

Anyway, he thought impatiently, he was no longer on visiting terms with the local dignitaries.

It would have sounded foolish in the extreme to suddenly enquire after a strange young woman he had only met for a few seconds in difficult circumstances!

He shivered as a cold draught from the ancient ill-fitting casement window swept under the dark red velvet curtains. He realised the fire had long gone out and it was very late.

The Earl picked up the papers and slipped them inside his thin black briefcase.

For some reason he did not want to leave them in his study or even lock them in the safe.

Their contents were crucial to the safety of several countries.

If they fell into the wrong hands or were read by the wrong eyes, just anything could happen in that sensitive geographical area, the Balkans.

He walked out into the cold echoing emptiness of the Great Hall.

As always the Earl felt a surge of appreciation and deep love for his home.

He ambled slowly through the Great Hall, admiring the beautiful tapestries, the collection of ancient spears and shields, the suits of armour his ancestors had worn in long ago battles, the stained and torn flags of the Regiment his family had given so many sons to over the centuries.

He had always been destined for the Army and he had enjoyed his time in India, serving his Regiment with bravery and distinction.

Then the blow had fallen.

His father had not even been ill, but caught a nasty chill out hunting one bitter January morning. The chill had turned to pneumonia and within a week he had gone.

He had received the astonishing and tragic news in India that he had inherited the castle and Somerton estates and fortune.

Although he had hated doing so, he had been forced to give up his Commission and return to England.

There he found the grieving Millicent, his father's young ward and he had no idea how to handle the problem of being in charge of such a young woman.

She had no relations and the castle was her home.

Marrying her had seemed the right solution to so many problems.

He knew in his heart of hearts that he had never loved her, but he had been very fond of the girl, although often exasperated by her light-hearted approach to life.

The Earl sighed.

He was well aware that he now had a responsibility to provide an heir to take on the castle and the estate.

He had no brothers or sisters with families and if he should die, the whole estate would pass to a distant cousin, who was living in some outlandish place in the Outback of Australia!

The future had seemed so easy and possible when Millicent had been alive.

Now – he could see no future for the family line at all.

He felt a surge of disgust at his predicament.

What was he supposed to do?

Marry some girl he did not know just to make her pregnant and produce an heir for the Somerton line?

It was a disgraceful idea, although he was sure that

some of his contemporaries would find nothing wrong with the plan.

Indeed the Earl was only too well aware that shortly after Millicent's death, the eligible daughters and sisters of friends had been paraded in front of him – as if they were in some sort of Arab bazaar and he was there bidding for a servant or slave-girl!

And people were wondering why he had now shut himself away in the castle, refusing to join in local Society!

High above his head in the darkness, a long wooden gallery ran around all four sides of the Great Hall, linking the vast round turrets.

The Earl found a candle and matches and holding the candlestick, he walked slowly up the polished stairs to the higher reaches of the castle.

This part of his home was in fairly good repair, but he had noticed a few days ago that the wooden posts of the long gallery skirting the East Turret had rotted away and there was a dangerous gap.

But luckily no one ever visited the East Turret and there was nothing there but empty bedrooms and attics full of centuries of junk.

This would be just the place he needed to hide his important papers far away from prying eyes.

The Earl edged round a clutter of broken wood and pushed open one of the attic doors. Just inside was an old walnut writing desk, badly damaged by water and damp in the past and left to rot, probably by his grandfather.

Carefully he put down the candle, pulled open one of the drawers, wincing at the squealing of warped wood, and placed the slim black leather case inside.

Then with a sigh of relief, he picked up the candle once more and returned to the corridor.

He felt exhausted, but knew that when he went to bed he would just lie there for hours, unable to sleep, his mind full of memories and regrets.

And sleep would never have come to him at all if he had known that Pardew had woken only a few minutes earlier from his drunken stupor.

Desperate for more brandy, he had set out towards the library where he knew there was a full decanter.

In the dark he had seen the Earl walking upstairs with a candle and intrigued had followed him.

And as the Earl hid the briefcase, Pardew watched him from the shadows, a sneer on his lips, and then slipped away before his Master spotted him.

*

Inside the ornate gold and turquoise bedroom in the South Turret, a soft and gentle snoring showed where Mrs. Rush had fallen asleep in her comfortable armchair.

The cook had sat by the young lady's bedside for hours, but apart from tossing and turning restlessly in her sleep, the girl had not woken and finally the long day had taken its toll on the plump Yorkshire woman.

Somewhere in the unfathomable depths of the great castle, a clock struck two and Jasmina woke with a start – she felt hot and desperately thirsty.

In her still fevered state she did not notice the water carafe on the bedside table.

Instead, she slipped out of bed, her feet silent on the thick rugs. The room was still spinning darkly around her, but somehow she reached the door and stepped out into the stone flagged corridor.

The sharp cold air now hit her fevered skin and she walked forward slowly, dreamily, almost unconscious, her temperature soaring.

Unknowing, Jasmina passed by the top of the great stairway in the dark.

Her bare feet were taking her straight towards the East Turret, the jagged edges of broken beams and a deadly plunge down to the stone floor below!

The Earl turned from closing the attic door behind him, when suddenly a movement at the end of the corridor made him look up sharply and the flickering candle jerked in his hand, sending mad amber shadows dancing across the old grey stones.

"A ghost! Damn it. I believe I have seen a ghost!" he exclaimed out aloud, almost laughing for the first time in months.

He had been brought up by his old Nanny with tales of a castle ghost – the Grey Lady, who haunted the upper passages after dark.

As a story to keep a mischievous small child firmly in his bed at night, it had not been that successful! The young boy had often crept out of his room when Nanny or his nursery maid had gone downstairs for supper.

He had wandered all round the castle in the dark, as sure-footed as a young goat, discovering all sorts of hidden doorways and passages, but he had never seen the famous ghost.

'All these years and I thought it was make-believe,' he chuckled to himself.

Then the laughter died from his eyes.

In the glow from his candle he could see that this was no ghost!

A young woman in a lace nightgown was walking slowly towards him and what was more terrifying, towards the very place in the East Turret where the banister rails were broken!

He could see bright golden hair cascading down her back and although her bare feet were hesitant in their steps, they were leading her slowly but surely towards her doom.

The Earl dropped the candle which blew out and hurled himself forwards.

"Stop! Wait! Do not move!"

Through the swirling heat of her fever, Jasmina was only aware of the dark all around her.

Then, just as she was about to step out into nothing but space, she was swept off her feet into two strong arms.

The Earl fell to the floor, clutching the girl with all his strength, his face buried in tresses of gold hair.

He felt his heart racing.

She had been within inches of *death*!

"Mary! Pardew! Hey, there! Someone! Come at once. I need help here! Mary!"

His clear voice rang out urgently through the silent castle.

Just at that moment there was a break in the snow clouds and the moon shone through a high window, its rays illuminating the couple locked in each other's arms.

Carefully he pushed the golden hair back from the girl's face as hurrying feet sounded from below.

Mrs. Rush appeared, scurrying along the corridor just as Mary came running from the direction of the West wing where the servants' living-quarters were situated.

"What the – " the Earl swore under his breath in astonishment, because he recognised the beautiful pale face beneath his questing fingers.

In the fitful moonlight he could see that lying in his arms was the very same young American girl he had last seen riding away on that great black horse!

Mary arrived carrying an oil lamp.

"My Lord, I can explain – "

"Oh, my dear Heavens, I must have fallen asleep," stammered Mrs. Rush, fanning her red face with her apron. "The poor child. Oh, thank goodness you stopped her, my Lord. She could have fallen to her death!"

The Earl climbed to his feet, still holding Jasmina in his arms.

"Explanations will have to wait. I take it from her attire that you have had this lady ensconced in a bedroom somewhere, Mary?"

The young housekeeper flinched at the tone of his voice and Mrs. Rush fell silent and backed away from the anger on her employer's face.

"Yes, my Lord," replied Mary quietly, refusing to show just how scared and upset she was. "George Radford found her lying injured in the snow and there was no way we could – "

"Which room?" the Earl interrupted, walking back along the corridor.

Mary hurried after him, the oil lamp swaying in her grasp.

"The Peacock room, my Lord."

The Earl felt his breath catch in his throat.

They had dared to give this stranger his dead wife's room!

When Millicent had been alive, the door between the Peacock room and the big Master bedroom had always stood open.

Since her accident, the Earl had moved to another part of the castle and had never been inside her room since the day of the funeral.

Without another word, he strode into the room and placed the girl gently onto the bed.

By the light of the oil lamps, he could see that she was very pale, but when he touched her forehead, it was hot and damp.

"She is running a fever," he said shortly. "We must call a doctor."

"But my Lord – "

"Pardew is still drunk and unconscious, I take it!"

"I – I – yes, my Lord, but George Radford is now sleeping in the scullery."

"Wake him and tell him to travel to the village and bring Doctor Meade here at once."

"But the snow – "

"The road from here to the village will be passable with care. We must get a doctor for this girl. Now go!"

Mary fled from the room.

The Earl spun round to Mrs. Rush.

"Tell one of the footmen to bring more coal up here immediately. We need a very good fire. She is desperately cold. And hot soup, Mrs. Rush. Chicken or beef stock and at once!"

The cook curtsied to him briefly and hurried away. She had not seen the Master so animated in years.

'Goodness, he looks incredibly like his father with his tousled hair and standing there in his shirtsleeves,' she thought, as she climbed down the steps to the servants hall.

The Earl turned back to the still figure on the bed. He picked up her hand and chafed at the pale fingers.

A lady's hand, that was obvious, but he could feel calluses made from leather reins. Indeed he had the same patches on his own fingers.

He reached across and smoothed the blonde tresses away from her face.

How big his hand looked against her cheek!

Suddenly he became aware that the girl's eyes were opening and she stared up at him, panic flaring.

"Don't worry about anything. Everything is quite all right. You are safe and I have sent for a doctor."

"I – I – I am scared. *Please*, do not leave me!"

The pale fingers tightened over his.

The Earl realised that she was almost delirious. He would have to humour her.

But his voice sounded deep and sincere as he told her,

"I will never leave you. Sleep now. You are quite safe here in my castle."

CHAPTER FOUR

Doctor Meade strode briskly into the Earl's study, pulling on his long black jacket over white shirtsleeves and a sombre mustard waistcoat.

Tall and thin and with a neat grey beard and side-whiskers, he accepted gratefully the glass of whisky the Earl handed him.

"Thank you, my Lord. Much appreciated on such a cold night – or should I say morning, because I believe dawn is now breaking."

"It was so good of you to come out, doctor. I have arranged for breakfast to be served to you immediately."

The Doctor raised an eyebrow.

It would hardly have been possible for him to have refused George's insistent demand earlier that night.

"And the young lady? What of your patient?"

The Earl turned away as he enquired and stood, one hand resting on the white marble mantelpiece, gazing at the embers of the fire as if the answer was of no consequence to him whatsoever.

"Luckily her fever has abated somewhat, my Lord. Your housekeeper dealt with the situation most promptly, it seems. The young lady is very strong with a most robust constitution and as long as she takes things easily for a few days, stays in bed and has plenty of nourishing food, then I see no reason why she should not make a full recovery."

"So in your opinion she should not travel?"

The doctor looked up sharply at the shadowed dark face.

"Certainly not, my Lord! That would be extremely unwise."

"Does she have a name?"

"It transpires that she is a Miss Jasmina Winfield, an American relation of the Duke and Duchess of Harley. She was on her way to visit other relations in Debbingford when misfortune overtook her."

The Earl frowned.

"Then surely I can arrange for her to be transported back to Harley Grange as soon as the blizzard stops? They will be most concerned for her safety."

The doctor shook his head.

"She was apparently travelling from Harley Grange to stay with these relations when the accident happened. The Duchess has gone to London – a grandson has arrived prematurely into this cold world, so it seems.

"So Harley Grange is empty and in my considered opinion, it would be unwise for Miss Winfield to continue her journey to the Parsonage at Debbingford, which I know to be extremely damp."

The Earl crossed impatiently to his desk.

"All right, Doctor Meade. You have indeed made your point. Miss Winfield must stay here at the castle. I will make sure she has every attention from my staff until she is fit to travel.

"Now, I will ring for someone to escort you to the dining room. I am sure you will be glad of some hot bacon and eggs before you have to venture out into the snow once more."

The doctor bowed, recognising that he was being dismissed.

"Thank you, my Lord. Most kind of you. Oh, and Miss Winfield is asking to speak to you. I said you would be up to see her directly. She should not be allowed to fret over anything at the moment."

*

Jasmina was dreaming she was running frantically through a blinding blizzard, her feet being held down by the soft clinging snow.

She could not see, could not hear – she was calling out for help, reaching out – desperately –

"Hush! I am here."

Her flailing fingers were grasped in strong hands and she sighed as she opened her eyes.

In the dim light coming through the open curtains, she could see a tall dark figure standing over her.

Immediately she knew who it was and why she was so disturbed.

"My Lord – forgive me – I should not be here! I must go at once."

"Miss Winfield! Please do calm yourself. What is this nonsense are you talking?"

Jasmina struggled to sit upright.

Mary stepped forward out of the shadows and slid her arm round the girl's slender shoulders.

"There, madam. Let me place this pillow behind your head." She glanced up at the Earl. "She is worried about being an unwelcome guest, my Lord."

"Thank you, Mary. Perhaps you should now go to the kitchen and ask Mrs. Rush for some hot soup."

Mary hesitated, then dropped a curtsy and left the room. The Earl loosened his grip on Jasmina's hands but stayed close to the bed.

"Miss Winfield, we do find ourselves in a very odd situation, don't we? We have not even been introduced, although I know the Duke and Duchess, of course."

"My Lord, I am so sorry to foist myself on your hospitality in this way. I now feel perfectly well enough to travel on to my relations in Debbingford."

The Earl frowned.

"Miss Winfield, that is not possible, I am afraid. The road out of the valley is closed because of the snow, and I do assure you, although I do not normally entertain houseguests, you cannot surely think that a stranger in my country would be turned away?

"I have heard that Americans shower their visitors with hospitality. Although I just cannot offer you any great excitement, you are welcome to the shelter of my castle until you are fully recovered. I have an extensive library, should you wish to read."

Jasmina's big blue eyes glistened for a moment.

Yes, she was indeed a stranger and in the moments of fever when she had come round during the night, she had longed to be at home in Missouri, in her own little bed.

But she now refused to show her aristocratic host her fears.

She raised her chin and faced him squarely without flinching.

"My Lord, I am well aware that you do not receive visitors here at the castle. Thus I do feel I am imposing on you."

The Earl suddenly wanted to smile at her and say that she was welcome to stay as long as she liked.

But that would be foolish.

He had no time for such social niceties, especially with stubborn, hot-headed young women.

"Not at all," he responded. "It is an extremely large castle, Miss Winfield, and there is no need for us to meet at all. Now I will leave you to rest in peace to recover your strength."

He bowed and left the room.

Jasmina stared hard at the closing door, a frisson of anger buzzing through her veins.

No need to meet at all! Well! She certainly had no need to speak to him again either.

Richard, the Earl of Somerton's ideas of courtesy and her own were clearly miles apart.

*

By lunchtime the raging blizzard had stopped, but the temperature had dropped and the snow was sculpted into weird and wonderful shapes, blown into peaks by the wind and frozen into fantastic ice mountains that looked like illustrations for some old book of children's fairy tales.

Mary, a heavy red shawl draped around her head and ears, slipped and skidded across the icy cobbled stable yard, a small wicker basket clutched to her chest. Inside, wrapped in a cloth, were two hot meat pasties and slices of cheese.

George Radford, the red-headed farmer she loved so much, was standing gazing moodily out from the stable entrance.

"I've brought you something to eat, George."

"Mary! You shouldn't be out in this cold, lass. But thank you kindly for the food. That'll go down a treat. I'm just about to head for 'ome. My old dog will think I'm not coming back, so I'll leave the pony 'ere. If I wear these snow shoes I found in the stables, I can cross the paddock and down through the woods. Snow'll not lie so heavy under the trees."

"The path to the village is clear, isn't it?"

"Well, it's passable with care. But no one's gettin' out of the valley over the pass just yet and that's a fact!"

"This heavy snow won't have done your old out-buildings much good," said Mary hesitantly, knowing how dilapidated George's farm was.

He worked every hour of the day to eke out a living from the poor land. There was never enough time to make improvements to the barns and sheds. And the farmhouse itself had a roof that leaked like an old bucket.

George was now strapping on his homemade snow shoes, round circles woven with cane that made odd shapes in the snow, but they would prevent him from sinking into the drifts.

He pulled his collar up round his ears that were already reddened by the cold.

"Aye, it's just what I have said to you many a time before, Mary. The farm's not in a fit state for a lass to live in. You'll just have to bide here awhile until I can do some repairs. Maybe next year – "

Mary bit her lip.

She knew only too well that there was no way the farm would be in any better state in a twelve-month.

She was already twenty-five, a confirmed spinster in most people's book.

"Don't you *want* us to marry, George?"

The young farmer turned and frowned at Mary, his hazel eyes bright with emotion under the thick thatch of his red hair.

"You know I do! I love you, Mary. But I'm not a-sellin' my land to that Earl and I 'ope he 'asn't been puttin' you up to talkin' to me about it again. I've said my final word on it. That piece of land has been in my family for generations!"

"But it's worthless – except to the Earl," declared Mary. "Two scrubby little fields which are under water for three months each year, plus half an acre of woodland and a run down house. The Earl will surely offer you a good sum, far more than all that is worth!"

George sighed.

He loved Mary dearly, but she did not understand. It was a matter of principle and the land belonged to him. Money was no use to him, he needed a home and a job.

In addition he knew he was angered by the fact that a man only a year older than he had so much privilege and wealth.

And why? Just because he had been born in the castle and not in a ramshackle farmhouse.

George had listened to several disturbing lectures recently by people who wanted to lessen the power of the upper classes.

He felt confused by all he had been told, but knew in his heart of hearts that a lot of the old ways were wrong and should be changed.

Mary watched him set off across the smooth snow-covered field and her heart went with him.

Then she sighed.

Her problems would have to wait.

She must return quickly to the castle and the young lady lying ill upstairs in the Peacock bedroom.

As she entered the warm kitchen, she was amazed to find Mr. Pardew, dressed in his overcoat and bowler hat, heading for the door with a big suitcase in his hand.

"Mr. Pardew? Where are you off to?"

The butler glared at her.

"I've just been a-given my marching orders, Miss

Landrey. That's what's happened! After all the years of service I've given to this family. It's a real disgrace, that's what it is!"

"You mean you've been given notice? But why?" asked Mary, although she had a good idea of the answer to that question.

Even now she could smell stale drink on the man's breath.

"Not in so many words. But I have been accused of drinking all the Master's brandy! Accused of being asleep when I should have been working. All lies, that's what it is. I don't think that young man is right in the head. So I'm not staying to be insulted like that."

"Mr. Pardew!"

The butler pushed past her.

"I told him so! 'Grief has turned your mind', I said. He told me to take a month's notice. Well, I'd like to see who he'll get to be butler up here in the wilds of nowhere. I won't even stay and work out my notice! I'm off and he can manage with you and that useless valet of his, Fergus. Now I'll bid you good day!"

And he stormed out of the castle kitchen, banging the door loudly behind him.

*

The day slipped past, dull and dark.

Jasmina slept, woke and sipped the nourishing soup Mrs. Rush provided and then slept again.

Around seven in the evening, Mary dimmed the oil lamps in the bedroom and went downstairs for her supper.

The click of the door latch closing behind her woke Jasmina from dreams of snow and clutching hands.

But she was overjoyed to realise that she felt much stronger and wide-awake.

She tried closing her eyes again, but now her strong constitution refused to allow another few hours' slumber it did not need.

'I cannot just lie here for another twenty-four hours pretending to be an invalid! I will go mad,' she thought to herself.

She pushed back the covers and pulled on a cream silk and lace dressing gown that had been laid on a chair next to her bed.

Then she padded across to the window and peered out into the night.

The moon was beginning to rise, gleaming on the snow-covered fields, hills and the moors rising up behind them, illuminating the countryside that would have been in total darkness without the blizzard.

'What a beautiful place,' sighed Jasmina. 'Oh, how I long to explore outside, but I suppose the doctor has told all of them to make me stay indoors in case my health is damaged. What rubbish. I feel quite strong now.

'Goodness, if I had a dollar for every time I fell off my horse back home in Missouri, I would now be a very rich girl!

'Well, at least I can explore the castle and stretch my legs a little. As long as I do not wander near the Earl's study, then I am sure that will be acceptable. After all, as he said himself, this is an extremely large castle!'

She hunted for some slippers, but could find none, so bare-footed, she left her room and walked slowly along the corridor, heading for the staircase.

At the very top of the circular stairway, Jasmina hesitated.

She was certain the Earl's study would be on the ground floor, so perhaps it would be much safer for her to explore the first floor of the castle.

She could see that the corridor heading towards the East Turret had now been barricaded to prevent some poor unfortunate servant girl from falling through the gaps in the banisters.

Jasmina turned, walked past the door to the South Turret where her bedroom lay and along the corridor that led to the West Turret.

Halfway there she paused.

A door was standing ajar and she could now see the flickering light from candles throwing shadows around the room.

She pushed the door open and stopped with a little gasp of surprise.

She was in a huge library where shelves contained books reaching up from floor to ceiling, the light gleaming off the gold lettering on the spines and jackets.

'What an amazing place!' whispered Jasmina as she glided over a large red Turkish carpet to inspect some of the treasures on oak shelves that had turned grey with age.

Obviously someone had been using the library quite recently, because a large leather-bound book had been left open on a small reading table.

Jasmina picked it up, running her fingers over the fine leather cover.

She glanced at the title – it was an academic work on the history of the Ottoman Empire – before replacing it carefully on the table once more.

She pushed the lamp further away from the book.

The flame was secure enough inside the glass, but with all the draughts and strange little currents of air that swirled round these ancient buildings, she knew you could not be too careful.

A fire in such a huge library would be disastrous.

Just as she was about to leave, her gaze fell on a piano in the corner of the room.

'Heavens! I have never in my entire life seen such a beautiful thing.'

She sat down on the piano stool and carefully lifted the heavily inlaid walnut piano lid.

Reverentially she ran her fingers over the black and white keys, delighting to find that the instrument seemed to be perfectly tuned.

Jasmina, like all American girls who had benefited from a good education, had learned to play the piano at an early age, but she had never been given the chance to try such a magnificent instrument.

Now as her fingers drifted softly over the keys, she was amazed at the beautiful sound it made.

'I wonder if the Earl plays. He did not strike me as the type of man who would have much time for music, but someone keeps this piano in tip-top shape.'

She let her thoughts drift away, back to her home in the United States, their big house in St. Louis, the music room leading out onto the shaded veranda and her Mama pouring iced tea for neighbours, who sat on the cushioned swing, gossiping.

Jasmina recalled a very jolly American folk song her dear Mama particularly loved and was about halfway through playing it, when –

"You play extremely well, Miss Winfield!"

Startled, Jasmina's fingers slipped on the keys and she looked up alarmed.

The Earl was standing right behind her, leaning on the back of a chair, watching her.

"My Lord – I am so sorry. Have I disturbed you? Oh, no, I suppose you have come to continue your reading. I will return to my room."

The Earl crossed to the piano.

"There is no need to. And please, will you stop apologising, Miss Winfield. Every time I see you, the first words out of your mouth seem to be 'I'm sorry'!"

Jasmina looked up at him, her eyes bright blue in the flickering candlelight.

"How incredibly boring of me! Well then, I will have to keep that phrase for an occasion when I may very well need to say it!"

The Earl smiled.

There was something refreshing about this girl. It was tempting to tease her, just to see how she reacted.

"Do you play, my Lord?"

"I have no time for games, Miss Winfield!"

Jasmina tossed her head, her golden curls tumbling across the cream lace dressing gown.

"I think you know, as well as I, my Lord, that I meant 'do you play the pianoforte'?"

The Earl's smile faded and he now reached across to pick up a small oil-painting standing in a frame on a side table.

"No, the piano was my wife's. I bought it for her – from Berlin. I hoped it would amuse her, but Millicent was such a carefree and energetic person. She always wished to be out-of-doors and on the go.

"She had no time for music, but I am certain that as she grew older, she would have loved music as much as I do."

"I believe your late wife was very young when she died so tragically, my Lord," Jasmina whispered.

The Earl sighed, the pain of his memories clear on his face.

"Yes, indeed. Millicent lived here from the age of

thirteen. She was my father's ward and when I inherited the title three years ago, we were married. She was just seventeen!"

He stood gazing down at the painting and silence fell in the room.

Slowly, carefully, Jasmina closed the piano lid.

"I am very well aware that the loss of a wife leaves a terrible scar, my Lord, and you have all my sincerest sympathies."

Abruptly the Earl put the little oil painting back on its silver easel.

Jasmina could see it clearly – a young girl with a cloud of dark curls, not pretty, but she had a charming and interesting face. If she had lived, she would have been an attractive woman.

But the artist had added a stubborn expression to her eyes and she wondered just how much resemblance the picture bore to the original girl.

The Earl pulled his mind away from many unhappy memories of a wife he had never understood.

It had been sensible to marry Millicent.

Indeed, he had thought he loved her, but knew now that it had only been affection he had felt.

One of his biggest regrets was that his heart had not been broken at her death.

He had been horrified at the waste, but more than anything, consumed with guilt that it had been his fault.

It had been most alarming for him to hear the piano music drifting down the stairways into his study.

Millicent had never had time to learn more than the few baby tunes she had mastered when a child, but this girl from America played quite beautifully and took full value from the piano that was still tuned regularly.

"I will leave you to your reading, my Lord."

Jasmina stood, pulling the cream lace gown tightly round her slender figure.

The Earl frowned and she wondered what strange English rule of manners or behaviour she had broken now.

Perhaps the robe was too flimsy to be worn outside her bedroom? But the silk was fairly heavy and the long lace sleeves and high neckline made it extremely decorous.

"You seem determined to injure your health, Miss Winfield," said the Earl, nodding towards the bare feet that peeped out from beneath the hem.

"Nonsense, the carpet is quite warm and soft, my Lord. I will come to no harm."

His dark eyes flashed with impatience.

"Good Heavens! If all girls from your country are as independent as you, then I pity your men folk! Listen, you have walked along a stone passageway to get here and unless you can manage to discover the secret of flight in the next few minutes, I expect that you intend to walk back again. You have had a severe chill and been extremely ill. Cold stones under your feet will do you nothing but harm."

"That, my Lord, if you do not mind my saying so is – *Oh*!"

She gasped as he stepped forward and swung her up into his arms.

Without another word he now carried her out of the library and back to her room.

Jasmina felt her world spin around her.

Her ear was pressed against his chest and she could hear the thump, thump, thump of his heart underneath his thin shirt.

Was it beating faster than hers?

She doubted it.

She had never felt so safe or secure in all her life as in the minutes she was held tightly by the Earl of Somerton before he placed her gently on her bed, bowed and walked away without a backward glance.

CHAPTER FIVE

During the night, the snow clouds had vanished over the frozen Yorkshire countryside and the moon swam up into the midnight sky as the temperature fell fast to below zero.

Jasmina awoke to a world hanging in a multitude of icicles, glittering brilliant white outside her window.

She could hear dogs barking and the sound of sheep in the clear crystal air.

A knock at the door heralded a little maid with big brown eyes, wearing a bright blue dress and white apron.

The pleated cap on her frizzy brown hair looked as if it was perched precariously on her head with the use of many hairgrips. She could have been no more than twelve years of age.

She was carrying a heavy brass coal-scuttle almost as big as herself and her face was scarlet from the effort.

She dropped a bob curtsy when she noticed that Jasmina was awake and proceeded to re-make the fire that had gone out over night.

Finally she sat back on her heels and announced,

"There, madam, that'll make the room snugger for you, I do reckon."

Jasmina pulled the heavy gold brocade cover round her shoulders and wriggled her toes in the chilly depths of the bed. Her breath was making little white clouds in the icy room.

Old English castles, she decided, were indeed most romantic places, but extremely cold in the depths of winter, that much was for certain!

"Thank you so much. That looks wonderful. What a good blaze. But I'm afraid I do not know your name?"

The maid smiled.

Gentry usually did not bother to find out the names of their servants, especially the housemaids who, with the girls who worked in the scullery, were the lowest ranked staff of all.

"I'm Florence, madam."

She picked up her coal-scuttle and headed for the door.

"Miss Landrey says for me to tell you not to 'urry getting' up. She will soon be bringin' your breakfast 'ere for you."

"Thank you, Florence. You are all being so kind to a stranger."

The little maid hesitated at the doorway.

"Be it true that you've a-come all the way from America, madam?"

Jasmina smiled at the awe in the girl's voice.

"Indeed, yes. My family live in a big City called St. Louis. It's right in the middle of America, a very long way away."

"Fancy that! And would there be Indians and wild men and bears and things, madam?"

"Well, many years ago, Florence, I expect that there were Indians. But not now. We do have a lovely big river called the Mississippi that runs through the middle of the City, and on the river are exciting paddle-boats that travel miles to lots of different places if you do not want to take a coach."

Florence's eyes were wide and bright.

"I'd just love to see that river, madam! Mississippi. What a very strange name! I've never even been down to London. But I went to York once with my Dad to see the Minster, which was very fine. I can't wait to tell 'im that I've spoken to a lady all the way from America. He'll be that pleased."

Jasmina laughed.

"Well, if your father would like me to tell him more about St. Louis, Missouri and the Mississippi River, then I will be delighted to do so."

"Oh, madam!"

The girl's eyes gleamed with delight.

"I'll let him know when I goes back to the village on my 'alf day. That I will."

A noise outside the door made Florence jump and she scurried out of the room just as Mary came in, carrying a tray.

She frowned after the small maid.

"I do hope young Florence has not been bothering you with all her chatter, Miss Winfield? We have so few guests at the castle that I am afraid she has not yet learned how to act in front of them."

Jasmina pushed herself up against the lace pillows as the room warmed from the now roaring fire.

"Not at all. She is so young and full of curiosity. Why, she is no different to the maids back at home who work for my family. I am sure they will want to know all the details of my trip to England when I get back to St. Louis."

Mary placed the tray on a small table and swiftly set out various dishes and a large pot of coffee.

"His Lordship has had his breakfast very early and is out checking on the stock. He is very anxious about the sheep. Everything froze solid last night and Mrs. Rush, our cook, is busy trying to thaw out the meat laid out in the pantry otherwise there will be no dinner for anyone!"

Jasmina now slipped out of bed and pulled on the beautiful silk and lace robe she had worn the night before.

Had the Earl really carried her in his arms along the cold stone corridor back to this room?

Or had it all been a wonderful dream?

'I would love to go out and explore after breakfast, but what can I wear?' she asked herself. 'I think the staff would look askance if I came downstairs in my negligee!'

Mary poured the coffee.

"Oh, George Radford has rescued all your luggage, madam. I will arrange for one of the footmen to bring it to you immediately."

Jasmina looked up, her blue eyes sparkling.

"How was it possible? Are the roads clear again?"

"Oh no. It seems that just before the blizzard came and brought down all the telephone lines, the Duchess sent word to her staff that, as you were spending Christmas with your relations in Debbingford, they should close up Harley Grange for the rest of the winter.

"Apparently she wishes to remain in London with her new grandson.

"Of course, Mr. Reid, the butler at Harley, thought that you had already reached Debbingford, so he had your luggage packed and the cart was dispatched. But then the blizzard came and the carter could only reach *The Golden Lion* in Somerton village. George discovered your trunks and cases there last night and brought them up to the castle very early this morning."

"That was very good of him," said Jasmina, eagerly spreading honey on her bread. "If only someone could tell me that my horse, Lightning, is safe and sound, my mind would be completely at rest."

"I am sure he will have found shelter somewhere, Miss Winfield. Animals have a strange way of being able to look after themselves when we cannot!"

"Do please convey my thanks to George Radford. Goodness, I have yet to tell him how grateful I am to him for finding me in the snow and bringing me here. Has he left the castle again?"

Mary now sighed and nodded and Jasmina noticed her pretty face had gone quite pink.

"He has his own farm to tend to. Not that he can do much in this bitter weather. Horrid little place, it be too. If only he would sell his land to the Earl – well! You'll not be wanting to hear all my silly gossip. I will send up your luggage immediately."

"Mary! Wait!"

Jasmina stood up, her curls falling in disarray over her shoulders.

"Why won't George sell his land? Will not the Earl give him a good price for it?"

Mary nervously fingered the big bunch of keys that hung from her leather belt.

"Oh yes, madam. His Lordship is a fair man and no one can ever call him anything else. He has made George a most generous offer for his farm, but there's no one as stubborn as a Yorkshireman when it comes to land.

"The Radfords have owned and farmed those few acres for many centuries, but it's a bleak damp corner of sour ground. This year even the turnips didn't grow well. The Earl would like to own it so he could link two big parts of his estate. He plans to drain the land and improve it.

"But George won't be budged, Miss Winfield. And

until he does, we cannot marry as there is no money to be had from the farm for him to support a wife and family!"

Then, as if she realised she had probably said too much, she nodded her dark head to Jasmina and swiftly left the room.

Jasmina finished her breakfast slowly, realising that she was extremely hungry.

She ate a boiled egg, drank her coffee and spread thick golden honey on soft bread, enjoying the good sweet flavour.

She had taken a great liking to Mary Landrey, the young housekeeper, and now guessed that her feelings for George Radford ran very deep.

Jasmina sighed and wondered what it would be like to fall in love with a man and to care for him so much that just to hear him speak would seem like Heaven on earth?

She wondered if that was how the Earl's poor wife had felt on her wedding day.

Had she loved him or had it just been a convenient marriage, necessary for the sake of convention when the old Earl had passed away?

Her luggage was brought into her room before she could ask herself why that should matter to her.

She carefully unpacked her very warmest skirt and jacket and found a pair of thick stockings and old leather walking shoes in the bottom of one of the trunks.

'Well, I will not look like a fashionable young lady, but I will certainly be warm!' she laughed as she inspected herself in the long cheval mirror that stood in one corner of the room.

Just as she was about to close the trunk, she noticed a package wedged down one side.

Why, of course! Her ice-skates! She recalled her

mother insisting they travelled to England with her, as she had heard that at Debbingford there was a large lake and there was sure to be skating at Christmas.

'I do declare that with this weather any local water will be frozen solid. I am sure the Earl must have a lake, too. An estate like Somerton is sure to contain all sorts of exciting things.

'If I cannot ride, then I will definitely skate instead. Goodness, I will go mad with boredom if I have to sit and read or sew all day until the snow melts. And obviously I cannot rely on the Earl for entertainment. He has made it very plain that I should stay out of his sight at all costs!'

Jasmina pulled on her heaviest cloak and made her way down the carved oak staircase into the vast central hall of the castle.

How wonderful it looked with the brilliant snow light flooding in through the small stained-glass windows, painting bright scarlet, blue and emerald patterns on the worn grey stones.

She could only stand and admire with awe the great tapestries, the suits of armour and the patterns of swords and sabres high on the walls above her head.

'It is all very marvellous, but all so very cold and severe,' she said to herself. 'Why, you could put some big blue and white bowls of flowers on those little tables and the whole place would look so much more cheerful and homely.'

Jasmina made her way down a narrow corridor and found a door leading into the garden.

She gasped as she pushed it open. The view was so beautiful.

She found herself standing on a terrace that had recently been swept and sanded and so it was easy to walk on.

A gentle snow-covered slope ran away behind the terrace down towards a line of willow trees.

Behind their bare branches that bent down towards the ground, Jasmina could see the silver glint of an ice-covered lake and beyond it rose the smooth slopes of the hills that led on to the wild moors.

"*Oh, how wonderful!*"

"You approve of the Somerton estate then, Miss Winfield?"

"Oh!" Jasmina turned, startled.

She had not heard the Earl approaching.

He was wearing riding breeches with high boots to protect him from the snow and a long, dark brown leather coat that snapped around his boots as he walked.

"Yes, it is marvellous. So wild and beautiful."

The Earl gazed out over the landscape that meant so much to him.

"I think you would like it even more in the spring. The fields are studded with daffodils and when the lambs arrive, you can see them playing in the pastures."

Jasmina sighed.

"Sadly, I will be home in Missouri by the time the daffodils appear. But are your flocks safe now, my Lord?"

"Yes, quite safe, thank goodness. I have very good shepherds. They brought all the sheep down from the high ground before the blizzard hit. They have a second sense as to when the weather is about to change."

"I heard dogs barking when I awoke this morning and the sound of sheep, but no voices. Your shepherds must work extremely quietly."

The Earl laughed suddenly, his serious face now looking much younger.

"I will tell them that, Miss Winfield. Although I think they would say that it is the dogs that do all the hard work, rounding up and guiding the sheep."

"I am anxious to explore. Would it be convenient for me to walk round the castle?"

The Earl nodded.

"Certainly. The terrace has been swept and sanded. It is quite safe."

He paused.

He was so tempted to walk with her and show this young American all the marvellous features of his home.

He was becoming intrigued by her high spirits and her determination to overcome all the difficulties put in her way.

Most aristocratic young ladies of his acquaintance would have taken to their beds for a fortnight after such an ordeal as Miss Whitfield had suffered.

But it was so vital that he finished the work he had intended to undertake when in London on all the Foreign Office papers.

As soon as the pass through the hills was cleared, he would have to leave on his difficult secret mission.

"You will excuse me if I do not accompany you?"

Jasmina found herself going red.

Goodness, surely he had not thought that she was angling for his attention?

Really, he was the most difficult of men.

One moment he would be laughing with her, his eyes warm and friendly and next the guard would come down over his face and he became a different person.

"I would not dream of imposing myself, my Lord," she said quietly, lifting her chin and meeting his gaze with a flash of blue eyes. "I shall explore where I can, perhaps visit the stables and take a look at your horses.

"And I can see that the lake over there is frozen. I have brought my skates with me and so I shall take a little gentle exercise on the ice. I can assure you that I have no intention of getting in your way. Good day!"

She turned to go and then started in surprise as his hand shot out to hold her arm.

"You must do no such thing!"

"I must beg your pardon, my Lord, but surely you can have no objection to my skating? I am not asking you to join me in what you could consider a frivolous pastime."

The Earl's face grew overcast with annoyance.

"The lake might not be completely frozen over. It is very deep in the middle and people have been known to fall through the ice."

Jasmina tossed her head, her bright curls dancing.

"I am not a complete fool, my Lord. I come from Missouri, an American State where it is far colder than this every winter.

"I am quite aware that I have to test the ice before I skate on it. Or do you believe that women do not have the same amount of common sense that men have?"

The Earl was losing his temper.

He was becoming convinced that the main problem with women was that their species were so over-headstrong that they could not recognise danger when it was right in front of them!

This young Miss Winfield had refused to dismount from that huge rogue horse when he had asked and look where that disobedience had led her.

He could remember so well another young woman who had also refused to take his advice.

He could see in his mind the horse being forced to jump over a fence that was far too high, the crashing fall, the limp body of his wife on the muddy ground, the end of all the hopes for Somerton.

Before he could think what he was saying, he heard himself speaking,

"I have no opinion on your common sense one way or the other, Miss Winfield, but maybe your manners could be questioned! I am particularly asking you not to skate on the lake today. Please accept my ruling on this matter."

Angrily Jasmina pulled her arm away sharply from his grasp.

How dare he call her ill-mannered?

"My Lord, I apologise if I have given you offence in any way. I am, of course, a visitor in your castle and country and will abide by all your rules. But, I can tell you now that if you were a visitor in my own home, I would not question your behaviour in such a rude fashion. Now, if you will excuse me, I find the air out here unbreathable!"

Her voice broke at the last word, but she refused to show him that there were tears burning in her eyes.

She spun on her heel and marched back inside the castle, shaking with anger.

*

A mile from the vast castle standing on top of its hill, the pretty little village of Somerton lay in a fold of the ground under a thick blanket of snow.

A few rooks circled lazily above the tall elm trees and the columns of grey smoke from the cottage chimneys rose straight into the freezing air.

A few children, laughing and shouting because the village school was closed for the day, were busy having a snowball fight and several housewives were hard at work, brushing the snow from their paths and steps, worrying about the water freezing in the outside pumps.

The sign outside *The Golden Lion* hung silent with no wind to make it squeak as usual.

Outside the temperature was dropping even faster again, but inside there was a roaring blaze in the immense fireplace and the air was thick with smoke and the smell of beer and roast beef.

George Radford sat in his usual corner, enjoying a pint of ale and a vast meat pasty.

When he had returned home from the castle, he had discovered that the heavy snow had brought down part of the chimney of his old farmhouse and until he could mend it, he was unable to cook on his range.

Mary had made him a big bacon sandwich when he had taken the American lady's luggage up to the castle, but that had been hours ago.

George now gazed into the fire and found himself wondering what it would be like to go home, cold, wet and tired and find Mary there, waiting for him with a cooked meal on the table and a warm loving smile.

He shook his dark red head and sipped his beer.

'No good dreamin' about such things, you fool,' he muttered to himself. 'You don't earn nearly enough from the farm to take a wife. Mary won't leave the castle to live in the farm and to be fair, it just ain't suitable for a lass and a family.'

George had left school when he was only fourteen to join his father working the land, but although he was not well educated, he knew in his heart of hearts that selling his land to the Earl of Somerton was the sensible thing to do.

But many centuries of independent Yorkshire spirit rebelled in him at the thought.

This was his land. He should hold it and pass it on to his sons, just like the old Earl had done with his great estate.

"Mr. Radford – may I have the pleasure of buying you a drink?"

George looked up, startled.

A tall thin man stood in front of him.

George could scarcely see his face under his black, broad-brimmed hat, but he could tell that the man sported a short dark beard and moustache.

His clothes were expensive, but the cut and colour told George that they had not been bought in England and that was a fact. And although the man spoke well, there was a trace of a foreign accent in his words.

George felt a spurt of suspicion.

This was right odd. How did the stranger know his name?

"No, thank you, sir. I'm just off home."

"Surely you have time for one more pint of the best bitter *The Golden Lion* can provide? Or perhaps a tot of spirits to keep out the cold? Come, I insist. I believe that I have a business proposition that will interest you."

"Are you a farmer, sir? Interested in buying some turnips, perhaps?"

The stranger laughed heartily, slapping his leather riding gloves against his palm.

"Turnips? No. I have another business altogether in mind. Listen to me, I have been told that you know a great deal about Somerton Castle. I appreciate that you are a busy man, Mr. Radford, but I would make it worth your while if you would sit and talk to me all about that great establishment."

He took a gold sovereign from his pocket and spun it on the table.

"You see, Mr. Radford, I, too, am a busy man. I am a student of architecture. I can study the outside of the castle, of course, but I would so like to know much more about the inside of that great building.

"For example, which rooms are where, how many doors lead from the main hall. Small things that I need to complete a paper I am writing for a Historical Society."

George ignored the gold piece, stood up abruptly, drained his tankard and placed it firmly on the table.

"Why don't you go up to the castle and ask to see round it, then? I'm sure that the Earl would be only too pleased to 'elp, if it's for some Society, as you say."

"Oh, I would certainly not wish to bother the Earl or his staff. Oh, no."

George silently pushed past the table, pulling on his coat and jamming his cap down over his ears.

He might well be in conflict with the Earl, but that was his business. There was no way he was going to talk about Somerton Castle to anyone, least of all some foreign outsider.

"I cannot help you, sir, and I'll bid you good day!" he said and strode out of the inn, letting a cloud of cold air rush into the muggy room.

The bearded man looked furious and turned to rap on the bar with the gold sovereign.

He ordered a large brandy and was standing sipping it, when the door opened again and Pardew, who had until that very morning been the butler at the castle, came in, his face like thunder.

"You don't look happy, Mr. Pardew," the landlord called to him, reaching for a glass. "Look as if you've lost a shilling and found sixpence. What's up?"

"I've been given my marching orders, that's what,"

he snarled. "That appalling young whipper-snapper who calls himself the Earl of Somerton.

"Oh, it's all right for the high and mighty Lords and Ladies to drink themselves stupid, but us poor fools who work for them aren't even allowed to have a quick sip of brandy to keep body and soul together.

"It's a pity we never had the revolution here like they did in France!"

The foreign stranger looked up, his eyes narrowing, as he pulled another sovereign from his waistcoat pocket.

"Sir, I am a stranger to these parts, but have quite a knowledge of revolutions in different countries. May I buy you a drink and perhaps hear your story?" he enquired.

The landlord watched uneasily as the man ordered two double brandies and led Pardew to a distant corner of the inn.

He harboured the oddest feeling that whoever this foreigner was, he was up to no good.

Outside *The Golden Lion*, George Radford paused and pulled the collar of his coat tighter round his neck.

The wind was still bitterly cold, freezing the snow as it lay and George trudged along the path that had been cleared around the inn and headed for the stabling at the back where he had left his pony.

It was time for him to return to his farm.

Not that there was much he could do there in this weather except make sure the stock were cared for, but stubbornly, he would keep trying.

In the stable yard, a young lad was walking a large black horse round and round, keeping him warm.

"That be a good-lookin' animal you've got there, young Joe," observed George, running his hand down the animal's neck, admiring the glossy coat and the fine arch of his head.

The horse danced away skittishly, fretting at the bit in his mouth and George reckoned he would be a devil to ride.

"Aye, belongs to a foreign gent just gone into the inn," replied Joe, controlling the horse, then, glancing over his shoulder to make sure no one was watching, he pulled something out from his pocket and showed George a half sovereign.

"Look at what he did give to me to keep his horse exercised!"

"Your lucky day, lad!"

George stared at the horse.

It was odd.

The saddle seemed far too lightweight for a man. It was made from a fine pale leather, more suitable for a lady.

As Joe started to walk on with the restless animal, George reached up almost automatically to straighten the saddlecloth that had become twisted underneath the horse's girth.

He felt a shiver run down his spine.

The saddlecloth was a deep dark blue and there, in the left corner, was a heavy gold embroidered crest.

And George was in no doubt who owned that proud mark.

This horse was the property of the Duke of Harley!

So why on earth was it being ridden by a stranger to the valley who possessed so much money to throw around that he could afford to give a stable lad *ten* whole shillings?

CHAPTER SIX

Jasmina spent the rest of the morning wandering through the castle, investigating chilly rooms that had been locked and left to the dust and spiders and others where she could tell that the servants had made at least some attempt at keeping up the appearances of a great house.

She did not envy Mary's job here.

It must be so difficult to motivate the staff when the Master of the house and estate obviously did not care.

To her amazement, Jasmina found a vast ballroom, its mirrors covered in white sheets, its once shining parquet floor dull and unpolished.

On the third storey she discovered what must once have been the nurseries and the schoolroom.

The bars on the windows, the quaint little pictures of dogs, horses and toy soldiers on the walls, left no doubt in her mind.

This was where the Earl had spent his childhood.

She found herself smiling – there were even small pencil marks on the side of the door where a little boy had measured his height every year.

He had sat at one of the desks with inky fingers and untidy hair, looking out over the lake towards the moors, probably longing to be outside riding his pony or running through the woods, climbing trees, swimming in the lake and having adventures.

Surely never in his wildest dreams would the Earl

have imagined that when the castle became his, he would order it to be closed up and neglected in this fashion.

The whole place just seemed to be sleeping, locked away from the real world.

'It's like a modern-day *Sleeping Beauty*, except his Lordship is no beauty! But – ' and she now sighed deeply ' – there is just no denying the fact that he is an extremely handsome man!'

She could see so clearly in her mind's eye the dark brown eyes that could command with a glance, the way he impatiently pushed back the black hair that flopped across his forehead when he least expected it.

Jasmina was quite sure that he was a man of great strength of character.

A leader of men.

There was far too much natural confidence in his bearing for him to be anything else.

So the reason for his withdrawal from Society must have been great indeed.

'He must have loved his young wife to the point of distraction,' mused Jasmina, running her finger along the dusty mantelpiece. 'It seems to me that he has been driven almost mad by her death.'

She was not certain as to why this fact made her so unhappy, but it did.

She returned listlessly to her bedroom, restless and unable to settle down to anything. She did not want to read or even play the piano.

In her luggage there was a tapestry bag containing the embroidery she had been working on, but having taken it out and after a few stitches, she threw it to one side.

She needed exercise, but it was really far too cold to just walk in the snowy grounds.

'Goodness, Jasmina Winfield, you are now turning into a terrified little woman,' she scolded herself. 'You are a free American with a mind of her own!

'You know very well that what you want to do is skate on the lake. It isn't going to do any harm to anyone if you spend just five minutes getting some exercise. You know you will be very careful and not come to any harm. I expect the Earl is shut inside his gloomy study, being sad, but there is no reason for you to follow his mood!'

With these brisk words she found her skates in the bottom of her trunk and hurried back downstairs.

With mounting excitement and trepidation, Jasmina made her way from the castle terrace, down a short flight of steep icy steps, through a border of old willow trees and down to the lake.

It stretched out straight in front of her, glimmering grey under the heavy sky. Smooth sheets of ice extended in all directions, clear across to the far side.

Jasmina brushed the snow off a wooden bench, sat down and changed her sturdy walking shoes for her heavy skating boots.

The brown leather was stiff and unyielding under her cold fingers, but eventually she managed to lace up the skates that had last touched ice so many thousands of miles away.

She shivered as the wind gusted across the lake and she knew that only a few minutes of skating would warm her up and bring a healthy glow to her cheeks.

But still she hesitated.

Had she really promised the Earl this morning that she would not venture out onto the lake?

No, she rather thought that she had said she would 'abide by his rules'.

Was that not the same thing as *promising*?

She bit her lip and clapped her cold hands together. She was far too honourable a girl to ever break her promise, but, oh, she did so want to skate!

Would it really matter, just this once, when the Earl would not even know?

'Jasmina Winfield, you know very well how much it would matter,' she murmured to herself and sighed.

No, she would not do it.

She had as good as promised and there was no way she would ever want the Earl of Somerton to believe that an American girl could not keep her word.

She decided she would sit by the lake for five more minutes and then go indoors and get changed.

It would be time for lunch very soon. Then perhaps reading a good book by a roaring fire was not such a bad way to spend such a miserable afternoon.

Just then a movement on the ice caught her eye.

There was the flash of a scarlet hood as if someone was sliding across the iced lake, not skating, but running and sliding, like a child.

Jasmina peered harder and realised that the muffled shape was quite small and, from the long skirt, it was a girl.

Perhaps she was a child from the village, sent up to the castle with a message and now hurrying to get home for her midday meal.

Whoever it was, she was very obviously enjoying herself.

But as Jasmina watched, disaster struck.

The child seemed to trip up – perhaps her foot had caught onto a half submerged log – and she fell headlong onto the ice.

Jasmina watched anxiously, but the figure lay very still, right in the middle of the lake where she knew the ice would be at its thinnest.

"Hello, over there! Are you all right?" she called, but there was no reply.

Desperately, she looked around for help, but there was no one in sight.

Well, promise or no promise, this was definitely an emergency and Jasmina could not leave the child lying on the ice. She could be badly injured.

Without thinking twice, she pushed herself out onto the cold lake and started to skate cautiously across to the motionless victim.

*

The Earl was sitting at the great leather-topped desk in his study, pretending to work.

In his shirtsleeves and waistcoat, he had a sheaf of important documents spread out in front of him.

These were the secret Government papers he had brought downstairs with him from their hiding place in the ruined East Turret.

He tried to read them, aware that, if they fell into the wrong hands, they could cause endless trouble abroad, especially in the powder keg countries of the Balkans.

The Earl realised that he should be concentrating on the notes and comments he had been asked to make based on the information he had been given, but his mind kept wandering away.

A pair of vivid blue eyes, cascading golden curls and a lovely but determined face just insisted on invading his thoughts.

A quiet tap on the door interrupted the pictures in his head and he thankfully called out,

"Come in!"

Mary appeared.

"Excuse me for interrupting you, my Lord, but will you be joining Miss Winfield for luncheon or do you wish for yours to be served in here? If you would wish to lunch in company, I will arrange for the meal to be served in the small dining room."

The Earl pushed back his chair.

"Where would Miss Winfield go to eat otherwise?" he asked dryly. "On the stairs? In the kitchen?"

Mary flushed.

"Of course not, my Lord. I will arrange for her to have a tray in her room."

The Earl hesitated.

He found to his total astonishment that he wanted nothing more than to sit opposite his young houseguest and talk to her about anything and everything that came into his mind.

But they had not parted on the best of terms earlier that morning and he had no doubt that she would prefer her own company at luncheon.

"A tray will do very well for both of us, I am sure, Mary," he said at last. "I see no reason for the staff to go to the trouble of heating the dining room and laying up a table."

Mary dropped him a short curtsy and left the room sighing.

Didn't the silly man realise that the servants would have been thrilled to have had something to do!

Mrs. Rush, for one, was becoming more and more irritated that her great culinary skills were no longer being appreciated.

Serving luncheon on two trays was not making any good use of such a fine cook.

The Earl was prowling around his study, picking up a book here, putting it down elsewhere, spinning the great globe until it squeaked and then slapping it shut with the palm of his hand.

He traced with his finger the outline of the United States of America and quickly found the City of St. Louis in Missouri.

Right in the very heart of the country. A very, very long way from England.

And soon Jasmina would be returning to her home and be no more than a memory. As he would be to her, no doubt. And not a very pleasant one!

He crossed to the window and gazed out.

Then he swore under his breath and strode furiously from the room, not even stopping to pull on a jacket over his shirt sleeves.

In the distance, he had caught sight a familiar figure skating off across the deserted lake.

Jasmina had defied him and was setting out onto the ice!

*

Jasmina skated slowly and carefully across the ice, aware that in places the colour of the ice was bluer and less solid, a sure sign that the water was not completely frozen.

When she reached the crumpled figure, she gasped.

A little face looked up from under the scarlet hood.

It was Florence, the young maid who had tended to the fire in her bedroom that very morning.

"Florence! Are you hurt, child? No, do not move. Let me see."

"Oh, madam, oh, dear. My ankle's got all twisted. Oh, it 'urts me somethin' real bad. Miss Landrey will be that cross with me. Oh!"

Her lament turned into a shriek as the ice beneath her, warmed by her little body, gave a sudden crack.

Jasmina caught her breath and tried to lift the girl, but she was too heavy.

"Florence, can you wriggle sideways – towards me. You must get off that piece of ice at once."

"I can't move my leg, madam! I'm tryin'. Oh, I'm ever so sorry. It be my afternoon off and I wanted to tell my Dad about you and America. Oh, my leg 'urts so bad. Oh, did you 'ear that crack? Leave me, madam. The ice is goin' to break. You'll go under too! Oh, whatever will his Lordship say!"

"Never mind his Lordship," Jasmina grunted grimly and flung herself flat on the ice, trying to spread her weight evenly over the wicked surface.

She knew that little Florence would have no chance if she was tipped into the freezing water. Nor would she, of course, but that was the furthest thought from her mind.

"Florence, now listen to me carefully! I am going to stretch out my hands and you must try to take hold of them and let me pull you towards me."

The little girl was sobbing now, but she tried to turn and reach for Jasmina.

But her thick coat was obstructing her and Jasmina cried out in horror, as another loud cracking noise sounded and thin lines in the ice began to appear around Florence.

"Whatever you do, don't move! You'll go through the ice. Let me pass," a familiar voice called frantically.

Jasmina gasped.

She had been concentrating so hard on the maid,

that she had not heard the swish of a sledge on the ice behind her.

The Earl was lying full-length on his stomach on a long wooden sledge.

He managed to manoeuvre it around Jasmina and with a huge pull from his strong arms, the little maid came slipping and sliding across the perilous ice to safety.

Later Jasmina could not remember clearly how they escaped from the lake.

She was vaguely conscious of the Earl leaping up and throwing himself and Florence towards the thicker ice as the wooden frame underneath him began to sink into the spongy surface.

The sledge was abandoned to its fate as the ice gave way finally and the inky black waters swallowed it up.

Carrying Florence under one arm and with a hand ready to steady Jasmina in case she should slip, the Earl brought them both back to shore.

Jasmina could only just recall the sight of Mary and Fergus standing horrified at the edge of the lake, ready to take Florence from the Earl and rush her back to the castle.

"Are you all right, Miss Winfield?" asked the Earl.

She nodded.

Her teeth were chattering too much to speak at first, and then she said,

"I am only cold and wet. My Lord, you are still in your shirt-sleeves! You will take pneumonia if you do not change into something warm."

The Earl ignored her.

"Sit on that bench and let me take off your boots," he ordered sternly. "Your fingers are blue with cold and you will never manage the laces on your own."

Jasmina did as she was told and sat gazing at the dark head by her knee as he knelt in the snow, tugging at the laces that were swollen and jammed by ice and water.

"You have saved both our lives today, my Lord," she whispered at last. "Thank you from the bottom of my heart. And I can only imagine how grateful that child's parents will be when they hear of her lucky escape."

The Earl glanced at her, his eyes dark with anger.

"I would not have needed to save anyone if the promise you made me this morning had been kept, madam! As for Florence, I expect that, if you had not interfered, she would have managed to crawl to safety. She is very light and her weight alone would not have broken the ice."

Jasmina caught her breath.

He was accusing her of contributing to the maid's plight.

"I do not expect you to believe me, but although I admit I did bring my skates down to the lake, I had decided firmly against venturing onto the ice purely out of courtesy to your Lordship.

"But when I saw her stranded, I could never have left Florence to her fate. The ice was already giving way when I reached her. Surely you must be able to see that I had no alternative?"

The Earl turned his attention to the other boot.

He could feel his temper rising again.

Jasmina Winfield would never know how terrified he had felt when he could see her lying on the ice, reaching towards his maid, the cracks in the ice radiating out from around their bodies.

He had thought she would drown and had known then that his feelings towards this young American woman, although confused, ran extremely deep.

He seemed to spend so much of their time together being angry with her, when all he really wanted to do was *kiss* her!

"Of course, if you tell me that is what happened, I would never dream of disbelieving you," he said, his voice stiff and formal as at last the final knot in the laces gave way.

Jasmina kicked off her skates and hurriedly thrust her cold feet into the walking shoes she had left under the bench.

She picked up her skates and shivered violently.

The afternoon was drawing to a close and the cold snow-laden wind from the moors began to blow once more across the valley.

"If you will excuse me, my Lord, I will go inside. I can only thank you again for saving my life for the second time.

"Let us both hope that soon the pass to Debbingford will be open and I can continue my journey to my cousins. I am sure you will be only too pleased to have your castle to yourself once more!"

And with a toss of her golden head, she turned and marched away back up the path.

The Earl watched her go, uncaring of the freezing wet shirt clinging to his body.

There was bravery in every step she took and he realised that he would never forget the sight of her trying to rescue the little housemaid.

Suddenly he recognised that he really did believe what she had told him – that she had not meant to break her promise.

And he knew she was too fine, too honourable to tell him otherwise.

For the first time in many years, Richard, the Earl of Somerton felt ashamed of his boorish behaviour.

*

Back in the castle, Jasmina asked a maid for a bath to be prepared with water as hot as possible.

She soaked herself in the bath for a good twenty minutes and was drying her hair in front of her bedroom fire when Mary knocked at the door and entered bearing a note on a silver tray.

Puzzled, Jasmina read it,

"*Dear Miss Winfield,*

I must apologise for my ungentlemanly behaviour earlier. I have a great deal on my mind, but that is no excuse to offend a visitor to my country, especially one as brave as yourself. Please accept this as an invitation to dine with me tonight."

And it was signed,

"*Richard Somerton.*"

Jasmina now looked up at Mary, her sapphire eyes sparkling and her wet locks clinging to her cheeks in little curls.

"The Earl has just invited me to dine with him this evening!"

Mary smiled.

"So I understand, madam. And quite right, too, you being a guest under his roof."

Jasmina crossed over to the dressing table, briskly rubbing her hair with a thick towel that smelt of lavender.

Reflected in the cheval mirror, she could see Mary hesitating in the doorway, almost as if reluctant to leave the room.

"I wonder, would you help me get ready, Mary?"

Jasmina asked impulsively. "I appreciate that it is not your job, but I am not sure if I can cope with my unruly mane alone.

"I could ask one of the maids, but I'm not sure if they have experience of putting up long hair for an evening and I do want to do justice to the Earl's invitation. If you are not too busy with other duties, of course."

Mary smiled at her, the frown lines between her eyes vanishing.

She liked this young American and, more than that, she liked the effect she was having on the Earl.

This was the first time Mary had known him show an interest in anything except for his silly old Government papers.

Even if it was only dinner, it was a start to getting him out of the clouds of despair he had been living in since his wife died.

"I would be delighted to help, madam. I used to do her Ladyship's hair every evening and I daresay I have not lost the knack."

Jasmina was tempted just for a moment to ask Mary about Millicent and then stopped.

She would have had no qualms on doing so back home in America, but she felt that it would not be tactful in these surroundings.

Jasmina smiled.

"There are dresses in that trunk, Mary, but anything suitable for dinner tonight with his Lordship must surely be creased."

"I will attend to it immediately, madam."

Mary opened the largest trunk and began taking out the clothes and laying them carefully on the bed.

It was lovely to drink in the vivid colours, touch the expensive fabrics, the luxurious silks and velvets.

There were evening dresses in pink, pale blue and white with matching shoes and gloves.

It had been a long time since such beautiful clothes had been on show at Somerton Castle.

"Which one will you wear, Miss Winfield?"

Jasmina was about to reply, then in the mirror she noticed the way Mary was stroking the velvet of one of her skirts and so she smiled to herself and pretended to fiddle with her hairbrush.

"Oh, you decide!" she said in an offhand tone. "I am sure you will know which one is the most appropriate. My jewellery box is in one of the trunks as well. We must choose something very suitable for this occasion, although I confess I do not own that many diamonds or emeralds to adorn myself with!"

She began brushing out her hair again, feeling a surge of excitement course through her veins.

This was a momentous occasion.

She was to dine all alone with the Earl of Somerton, the man who constantly invaded her thoughts and dreams, the man who had saved her life twice.

Jasmina remembered her last day at Harley Grange as she looked out of the window at Somerton Castle.

She recalled listening to the Duchess's gossip and wishing that she could meet the Earl who sounded such a romantic tragic figure!

Well, she had met him and she was going to spend an evening in his company.

This surely was the most important day of her life!

CHAPTER SEVEN

At eight-thirty precisely that evening the Earl was standing, a glass of sherry in his hand in the drawing room of Somerton Castle.

He had hesitated before donning his dinner jacket, but finally decided that the occasion merited it.

When the door opened and Jasmina Winfield was announced, he felt a thrill run through him and he was glad that he had made the effort.

The American girl looked superb.

In point of fact he could hardly recognise her from the figure wrapped in coats and shawls he had argued with so vehemently only an hour or two ago on the banks of the frozen lake.

Her shining golden curls were piled on top of her head in a very elaborate style, laced through with dark pink ribbons. Her dress was matching dark pink velvet, slightly off the shoulder, but fitting tightly into her tiny waist.

She was wearing a gold and pearl link necklace and bracelet and tiny gold and pearl studs in her ears.

The Earl found himself wondering how she would look with rubies and diamonds against her creamy skin.

Then he shook himself.

This was madness!

The girl was just a passing guest at the castle and an annoying one at that!

Very soon she would be heading off to be with her relations in the next valley and later she would be returning to her home in America.

This dinner was just by way of an apology for his abrupt behaviour earlier – nothing more.

"*Miss Winfield!*"

He reached out to take her hand in his, aware of the strength in her fingers that looked so fragile.

"Let me pour you a glass of sherry. I hope that you have fully recovered from your adventures on the ice?"

"Could we dispense with the formality, my Lord? I am sure there is no one around who would be offended if you called me 'Jasmina'."

His dark eyes gleamed suddenly with amusement.

"My ancestors would be shocked and I am certain that the servants would disapprove, but if I am to call you 'Jasmina', then you must use my name – 'Richard'."

"Yes, my Lord – I mean Richard!"

As she smiled up at him, the blue of her eyes took his breath away.

"It was kind of you to accept my invitation to dine. I could not have blamed you if you decided never to speak to me again after my boorish behaviour earlier."

Jasmina blushed and sipped her sherry.

She was sure it was the alcohol that was making her heart beat so fast. She was not used to anything stronger than champagne.

"I am sure you were only trying to protect me. But I am afraid American girls are not like English ones. We are trained to look after ourselves and stand on our own two feet."

The Earl smiled.

"I am rapidly becoming more and more aware of the

character of young American women, Jasmina! But I am afraid it is bred into me to protect the fairer sex at all costs."

She smiled and asked,

"Have you heard how Florence is progressing?"

"Indeed, I had a report a few minutes ago that she is well on the way to recovery. Her leg was badly twisted, but she has youth on her side and will soon be up and about again."

Just then the door opened and Mary appeared.

"Dinner is served, my Lord," she murmured.

The Earl held out his arm and with a smile, Jasmina placed her hand on his wrist and walked with him through the connecting doors into the castle dining room.

She gave a little scream of delight.

The room was situated in one of the castle's turrets and so was completely round. Tall tapestries decorated the grey stone walls and bright Turkish rugs covered the floor in a myriad of blue, ruby and emerald colours.

A cheerful fire was burning in the hearth with the logs crackling, keeping away the chill.

Heavy red velvet curtains were drawn across the deep windows, shutting out the snowy night scene.

A small round table had been laid, sparkling with white china rimmed with gold, crystal glasses, solid silver cutlery and, in the centre, a deep bowl of white lilies and sprigs of holly, the berries bright red against the flowers' white petals.

"Someone has just gone to a great deal of trouble," smiled Jasmina, as a footman moved her chair back.

The Earl nodded.

"I fear I am a sad disappointment to my staff. I do not entertain. This is the first chance they have had for a great while to show me their varied talents."

Jasmina slowly sipped the delicious *consommé* that had just been served to her.

"Are you averse to entertaining as such, or is it just the lack of neighbours that prevents you?"

"I must admit that there are only a few people that I admire living locally. I do not hunt and only shoot for the castle's larder. So you see, Jasmina, in the eyes of Society, I am an abject failure."

Jasmina was silent as a superb dish of Dover sole in champagne sauce was served.

When the footman had left the room, she glanced across the table at the Earl's face.

He was frowning as he pushed the fish around on his plate.

She wondered if he was thinking once again about Millicent, the girl who had stopped his life in its tracks.

Well, she decided, if she wanted to know, there was one sure way of finding out!

"Did you entertain much when your wife was alive, Richard?"

The Earl's fork clattered noisily onto his plate and he glanced up at her, his eyes dark.

Unbidden memories came flooding back.

He recalled the crowds of youngsters who had often stayed at the castle for weeks at a time. Rich, idle, little more than children themselves with too much time on their hands, only interested in enjoying themselves.

"Millicent boasted many friends. People very like herself – all young, eager for excitement and adventure, unwilling to listen to advice."

Jasmina took a sip of a clear golden wine.

"You very much sound as if you disapproved of her behaviour."

The candles flickered in a draught from the door as the footman came in to clear the course.

The Earl watched moodily as a confection of apples and cream was placed in front of them.

He could not believe how blue and direct Jasmina's gaze was.

She appeared to be challenging him and there was nothing retiring about her presence at his table. The tilt of her pretty chin, even the way she sat at table, upright and determined, was so different from the languid young ladies whom he had met recently.

"She was my wife and – " his voice roughened very slightly, " – so young to be a Countess. I am sure that, had she lived, she would have taken on the various duties and responsibilities of the first Lady of Somerton. But – " and pain tore through him, " – she did not live and that was my fault!"

Jasmina gasped and instinctively reached out across the table to touch his hand.

His fingers twined with hers and she felt a quiver of emotion run through her body.

"You blame yourself for her death, Richard?"

The Earl looked at her, his eyes shadowed by his dark thoughts.

"Millicent loved riding above everything else and she loved to hunt. While I was staying away in London, she purchased a new horse from a dealer I did not trust. I begged her to think again, but she would not."

There was a little silence. Jasmina was tempted to speak, but something held her back. She had the feeling that if he did not tell her now, he never would.

At last the Earl continued,

"The horse arrived, but it was scarcely broken in, a chestnut, a wild creature, although good-looking in a flashy way. Probably with calm patient schooling it would have become a fine ride. But Millicent was not a patient type of girl.

"She had invited some of her young friends to stay at the castle for a weekend party."

He passed his hand over his eyes, as if wishing to wipe away the memory.

"At breakfast that morning she announced that she would show everyone what her new horse could do over the fences. I begged her, I pleaded, and finally I *ordered* her not to be so stupid and rash."

Jasmina frowned.

"She did not listen?"

He laughed and it was an unhappy cold sound.

"Indeed she did not. She told me that I was an old-fashioned fuddy-duddy if I thought she was the type of old-fashioned wife who was going to obey her husband's every command.

"She insisted she was an extremely good rider and she would show me and everyone there just how silly I was to try and stop her. Then – "

"Hush! You need say no more!" Jasmina broke in swiftly. "But Richard, as dreadful and tragic as her death was, in no way was it your fault! She was a young girl, probably spoilt by you and your father, whom I have heard doted on her when she became his ward. She went her own way and it led to her untimely death. But you are *not* to blame."

The Earl looked across the flickering candles into her blue eyes.

"I should have been more forceful," he said quietly.

Jasmina sighed.

"Richard, unless you had locked Millicent in her turret room, I cannot see that you could have stopped her!

Women are different these days. We make decisions for ourselves and sometimes they are the wrong ones, but the fact that we make them ourselves is still important."

He stared at the fearless expression on her face.

Yes, this young American had a strong independent streak running through her. Why could she not see that in this modern world it could lead her into great danger?

Although he believed Jasmina when she told him she had not intended to go out onto the ice this afternoon, she had still done so when Florence fell over.

And she could easily have drowned in the freezing waters of the lake.

"So you would have done the same thing? Gone against all my wishes?" he enquired slowly.

Jasmina pushed her plate away.

"Well, I would like to think that I would not have been deceived by the bogus horse-trader in the first place! But at your poor wife's young age, with no real knowledge of the outside world and taking everyone at face value, then maybe I would."

"And obeying your husband? Would that not be a rule you lived by?"

Jasmina reached out her hand and began to toy with the lilies and holly leaves of the table decoration.

"Love, honour and obey, is not that what every wife promises at the altar?" she replied thoughtfully. "I hope I will do everything in my power to keep that vow when I take it.

"I believe I would never marry anyone I could not trust implicitly, but I cannot obey a man whose commands are wrong. God gave us all common sense and everyone, even women have to use it!"

The Earl pushed back his chair and stood up.

But the force of his movement slid the contents of the table to one side and Jasmina grunted with pain as a holly leaf cut into her finger.

"You are hurt!"

"No, it is nothing."

"Let me see?"

He smiled suddenly.

"And that is a request, not an order!"

She raised her hand and he took it gently, bending his dark head to examine the pearl of red that was welling up from where the thorn had pierced her skin.

Taking a handkerchief from his pocket, he dabbed the blood away.

"I think you will live!"

Then a look of pain swept across his face and she knew he was remembering the girl who had disobeyed him and died as a result.

She stood up, raising her gaze to find him staring intently down at her face.

His grasp on her hand tightened and she swayed forward.

His lips were so close and she knew he was about to kiss her and she was going to let him.

Then just at that very moment, the door opened and Henry, one of the castle footmen, appeared bearing a pot of coffee on a silver salver.

Jasmina pulled herself away, knowing her face had gone as pink as her dress.

"I – I must go and wash my hand, my Lord," she stammered. "Thank you for a – lovely dinner. I will not take coffee as I fear I shall not sleep if I do."

Without a glance in his direction she fled from the

room, picked up the long velvet skirt of her dress and ran up the stone steps.

She did not stop running until she had reached the sanctuary of her bedroom.

Jasmina closed the door behind her and stood with her back against it.

Goodness, what could be wrong with her?

Running away like a stupid schoolgirl because a man had looked as if he were going to kiss her!

'But this is *Richard*,' she whispered to herself as she sank down onto her bed.

And that was the problem.

She had to recognise the dreadful truth – she was falling in love with him.

A lonely widower who did not want another wife, who thought all women should know their place and obey every order their husbands gave them.

How could she, Jasmina Winfield, fall in love with this dark unhappy man who was so rooted in his past?

What could she – a young woman from the New World – possibly offer him?

It was hopeless.

Why, she would be on the other side of the Atlantic Ocean in a few weeks' time. After Christmas, she only had a few more days to spend in Yorkshire and then she would be travelling back to London to board a ship and head for home.

But as she buried her face in her pillow and let the tears fall, Jasmina knew that for all her brave resolutions, how she felt about the Earl could not be denied.

*

Down in the castle's kitchen, Mary and Mrs. Rush, were finishing their supper.

There had been plenty of *consommé* and Dover sole left over and they had enjoyed every mouthful.

The rest of the staff were all sitting in the servants' hall, but the two senior female members of the household boasted the luxury of a little side room that Mrs. Rush kept for herself.

"Did the Master and Miss Winfield enjoy the meal, do you think, Mary? Not much came back to the kitchen, that's for sure."

Mary frowned.

"I think so, but the young lady did not stay to take coffee with the Master. She went up straight to her room and Henry says he thought she looked a bit upset when she passed him."

Mrs. Rush sniffed and folded her arms across her amble bosom.

"Now, Mary, you know I would lay down my life for his Lordship, but I have to say I don't have any great regard for his common sense. All this moping around over her Ladyship's death. It was an accident, fair and square. He ought to move on."

"She was far too young to marry the Earl and settle down to all that responsibility and so spoilt by the old Earl and his Lordship when he came back from India. Now this American lady – "

Mary raised her eyebrows and Mrs. Rush nodded in agreement. Although they would never dream of gossiping about it, they could both now see that Miss Winfield would indeed make a marvellous Countess.

At last with a wide yawn, Mrs. Rush heaved herself out of her chair and announced she was off to her bed. She would be up at five o'clock to start another busy day.

Mary said goodnight and spent a few more minutes working on her household accounts. Only Henry was still on duty because the Earl had remained in the library and might need him.

Just then a bell on the board above the kitchen door rang.

Henry looked up and scowled.

"Front door? Who can it be at this time of night?"

"You'd better go now and answer it," said Mary, puzzled. "Before the Master starts ringing down asking what is going on."

She sat, pencil in hand, until Henry returned.

"Well?"

"A visitor for his Lordship. Foreign gent. Seems very pleasant. I told him that the Master was not receiving callers, but he insisted I take his card in anyway.

"He must be someone the Master knows because he read the card and told me to bring him to the library. Then his Lordship said he wouldn't need me any more tonight. I'll be glad to get to my bed."

"What a strange time to call! Did you get his name?"

Henry shook his head.

"It was a long, foreign sounding one, that's all I can remember. And he mentioned that he'd been delayed by the weather. Reckon he couldn't have come far, though, because his cloak was quite dry."

Mary shook her head.

The strange ways of the gentry could be confusing sometimes. But then if the visitor was a foreigner, it was even weirder – in Yorkshire at this time of the year!

Still the Earl asked to see him. That was surely a good thing.

Why, what with the dinner with Miss Winfield and accepting a caller, things at the castle were looking up!

She put out the oil lamps and made her way silently through the great echoing hall to check that Henry had put the bolt on the front door.

Sometimes he forgot to do so and although no one was likely to burgle the castle, Mary always wanted to be sure it was quite secure.

She went back down the long passageway that led to the kitchens, through the green baize door, then jumped, her hand going to her throat.

A man was standing by the scullery door.

"Mary?"

"George! What are you doing here so late? You nearly made my heart stop. I thought you were a burglar."

The red-headed farmer grinned at her and pulled her close for a kiss.

"Sorry, Mary, pet. I didn't mean to scare you, but I saw somethin' real strange today down at *The Golden Lion* and thought you should know."

They sat at the kitchen table, holding hands across its white scrubbed surface and George told her about the foreign bearded man and the horse he was riding that had obviously come from the Harley stables.

"But what do you reckon that means?" she asked.

"I think it be the mount Miss Winfield were a-ridin' when she 'ad 'er accident. I can well see 'ow she was thrown as the 'orse just bolted and to be fair, this stranger might have found the animal wanderin' in the storm. But if that was so, why didn't he 'and it over to the authorities when the blizzard stopped?"

Mary bit her lip. George was right. It was all very odd.

She made up her mind.

"The Master has a visitor at the moment and it will be too late to disturb him when the gentleman leaves. But tomorrow morning, first thing, I'll go and tell him," she said firmly. "He'll know what to do."

George yawned.

"Right, that's fine with me. You tell 'is Lordship. I don't want to speak to him."

Mary's big grey eyes shone with concern.

"Perhaps if you two could just sit down and discuss your farm sensibly – "

George stood up abruptly.

"No, Mary. I don't want to argue with you, but I'll not give up my 'ome, a place that's been in the family for generations, for a purse full of guineas. I've as much right to own land as the Earl of Somerton!"

With that he strode across to the back door, opened it and groaned.

"Damn! It's snowing again! I wanted to take the pony home with me."

"Bed down, George, in the scullery again. It might have just stopped by tomorrow morning."

Mary smiled mischievously.

"And I like seeing your ugly face over the breakfast table in the morning!"

And with another kiss, she left him and headed for her room.

*

The cold woke Jasmina from a restless doze. She realised she was shivering, still lying on top of her bed, wearing her dark pink evening dress.

She had cried herself to sleep, but she could tell from the little clock on the dressing table that it was only about two in the morning.

She got up, lit the oil lamp and took off the gown she

had donned with such high expectations earlier.

How could she possibly have been so stupid as to fall in love with the Earl of Somerton?

That way lay great heartache because she was quite certain he would never ever consider her a suitable wife!

And that was even if he wanted to marry again and she was convinced that he did not.

Jasmina peered out of the window.

It was snowing again – great fat flakes that settled silently on the already icy ground.

She pulled from out of her trunk an old dark blue dressing gown she had brought all the way from her home in Missouri.

It was far shabbier than the wonderful concoction of silk and lace she had worn since her arrival at the castle, but she had no longer any wish to wear anything that had belonged to the Earl's first wife.

Jasmina brushed her hair and tied back the unruly curls with a length of blue ribbon.

She did not feel at all tired.

Indeed, she had to admit that what she did feel – apart from a great unhappiness – was hungry!

She glanced at the bell pull by her bed, then shook her head.

'No, I cannot possibly wake up some poor servant just to get me something to eat!' she murmured to herself. 'That would be so unkind.'

But the more she thought about her needs, the more desirable a drink seemed. A cup of hot milk would make her feel so much better.

Jasmina had no fear of the dark.

She knew there was always a lamp left burning in

the Great Hall and there would be plenty of candles in the kitchen.

Impulsively she tied the girdle of her dressing gown tightly round her waist and slipped out of her room into the dark corridor.

As she padded silently along towards the stairway, she wondered exactly where the Earl slept.

Was he asleep? Or was he wide awake as well and ruminating about Millicent and the guilt he carried for her death?

As she reached the turn of the stairway that swept down into the Great Hall, a sudden noise made her stop.

For some reason, the noise seemed all wrong.

There were always plenty of odd sounds in very old castles of course – wood shifting, mice scrabbling behind panelling, draughts lifting the tapestries from the walls and then dropping them with gentle little thuds.

But this noise had been – *different*.

Then, almost at once, a dim light appeared from the direction of the Earl's study.

Jasmina gasped and shrank back against the wall in the deep shadow.

She could not bear to speak to the Earl again this evening.

Not until she had a chance to regain her composure and could pretend that he meant nothing at all to her.

She would die of embarrassment if he guessed she had any feelings for him.

As she watched, her blood ran colder than the stone flags beneath her feet.

Three burly men came out of the Earl's study – two of them were half carrying Richard between them!

105

The Earl seemed dazed and was stumbling, as if he had received a blow and was half unconscious.

Another tall man in a dark cloak was holding a thin black briefcase in his hand.

By the light from the small oil-lamp on the table in the hall, Jasmina could see that he had a small black beard and the thin lips behind it were smiling.

He moved swiftly to the heavy front door and slid back the bolt.

Then before Jasmina could even think, the door had swung open and the four figures had vanished out into the snowy night.

CHAPTER EIGHT

The main door to the castle had just closed behind the gang of men carrying the Earl away when Jasmina sped down the stairs and opened it again, just a crack, enough to look out.

To her horror, she saw the Earl being lifted onto a horse, held steady by one of the ruffians.

Another man was leading the animal away, cursing vilely as he slipped and slid on the icy ground beneath the freshly fallen snow.

Jasmina nearly cried out in astonishment.

The dark bearded man had mounted a large black stallion that was pulling at his tight reins, hooves trying to find a purchase on the ice.

She would have recognised that horse anywhere.

It was her *Lightning*!

And suddenly her memory came flooding back and she could remember it all –

The Earl almost running her over in his car, arguing with him, then riding hell for leather through the woods on the way to Debbingford –

Men leaping out at her from the trees and grabbing Lightning's reins – being thrown –

And the man's face who had stolen her horse!

"Oh, my goodness! Oh, Richard! I must get help. The Earl is being kidnapped!"

She fled back up the stairs, gasping for breath, then up another flight until she reached the wooden stairs that led to the staff quarters.

In desperation she hammered on Mary's bedroom door until it was flung open and Mary stood there, her hair tumbling over her shoulders, looking alarmed and worried.

"Miss Winfield! Whatever can the matter be at this hour? Is it a fire?"

"No, raise the household, quickly, Mary. The Earl has been kidnapped!"

"*Kidnapped*?"

"Yes! Yes! Oh, do come. We must send for help. We must follow them. There is not a moment to lose!"

"What's all the rush and bother? Waking a woman out of her sleep."

It was Mrs. Rush, coming down the corridor with a heavy tread, wrapped up in a vast grey woolly gown that gave her the look of a small cuddly elephant.

Other doors now opened and several maids, Henry and Fergus appeared.

Voices were raised and for a few moments all was confusion and noise.

Jasmina effortlessly took control and made herself heard over the babble.

"Mary – you must send for help from the village. The telephone line is down, I know, but we have to raise the alarm. The Constable must be informed at once and he will know what to do. I'll go downstairs and check on the tracks. If we do not discover the direction they are headed, we will never find him!"

Knowing she could leave Mary in charge, Jasmina fled back to her room and dressed speedily into her leather riding trousers and oldest boots.

She barely had time to pick up a thick jacket to pull over her woollen top and then she was running downstairs, through the hall and out into the freezing night.

She stared down at where the snow had been kicked up and disturbed by men and horses.

The hoof marks were already vanishing under the fresh white blanket. Soon there would be no sign of which way the kidnappers had gone.

Jasmina looked around her in despair.

There was no one in sight and the falling snow cut her vision to only a few yards.

'What can I do? Oh, Richard, Richard, surely they would not harm you? But such violent men. Anything could now happen and I know I will die, too, if anything dreadful befalls you.'

Every emotion she was feeling came swirling to the surface and her heart felt as if it would break.

But now was not the time to give in to despair.

Jasmina had learnt from the farmers back home that tracking people through snow was a risky business as the wind could wipe out everything in seconds.

'Every minute we lose is precious. There is no time to wait for help from the village,' she thought desperately. 'If Richard is to be saved, I must do all I can to help him.'

She fought back the tears that threatened to sweep down her cheeks.

It was only now when she was in danger of losing him that she finally admitted to herself how deeply she had fallen in love with Richard, the Earl of Somerton.

It was a love that would never be returned, Jasmina knew that. But that did not lessen its depth.

She had known from the very second Richard had caught her in his arms that fateful night she had nearly fallen to her death from the gallery that her heart belonged to him.

'And now I must try and save him!' she murmured. 'But I must hurry! They have already a good start but, oh, Lord, I will never catch them on foot.'

An idea flashed into her mind and she turned and sped along the terrace that surrounded the castle, her heart thumping, her mind consumed with terror for Richard.

Would they hurt him? Would they perhaps demand a ransom? Kidnappings were commonplace in America, but Jasmina had not realised they happened in England too.

But if they had taken the Earl to demand a ransom, who was there to ask? He had no immediate family.

Random thoughts scurried through her brain.

Was he badly injured? He seemed stunned when she had seen him and he needed to be carried and dragged outside.

'But perhaps he was just pretending,' she cried to herself, 'to slow them down and give himself a chance of being rescued.'

She could only hope she was right.

And just who was the bearded man who had stolen Lightning and seemed to be in charge of these dire events?

The castle stables felt warm from drowsy horses and Jasmina knew full well that it was pointless taking one of the spirited thoroughbreds for a task like this.

She had seen earlier how difficult Lightning was to handle with the ice under his hooves.

No, she required something plainer and stronger – and there was George Radford's stocky grey pony, still in the Somerton stables, waiting to be taken back to the farm when the weather improved.

Swiftly she led him out.

Jasmina had learnt to ride bare-backed on the plains of Missouri and a small pony was no problem for her.

Even as a young groom stumbled out of his room, rubbing his eyes in amazement to find the American lady in the stables in the middle of the night, Jasmina acted.

Not bothering to call for a saddle, she pulled on the pony's bridle and, in just a few seconds, had vaulted onto his wide grey back and was urging him down the path.

Gathering all her strength, she now settled down to follow the kidnappers' tracks and sent up a fervent prayer of thanks that she had regained all her strength following her last disastrous outing on horseback.

*

Back at the castle, all was uproar in the kitchen.

At the calm centre of the storm stood Mary, issuing orders in a low sensible voice that cut through the noise.

She sent Henry to the village to fetch the Constable.

Fergus had wanted to rush after the kidnappers, but Mary stopped him.

"Listen, Fergus, the Constable cannot possibly hunt these men down by himself. I need you to go to as many farms and cottages as you can reach and rouse the men. Tell them to meet up in the village and the Constable will know what they can do."

She swayed a little and gave a little sob as George's strong arm supported her.

"Hold up there, Mary love," he urged. "We need you to be strong for us all."

"I know and I will. But oh, George, I believe Miss Winfield has gone after them! I swear I did not know. I thought she was just going outside to see which direction they had taken, but she hasn't come back!"

George gave her a hug.

"Now, now, that's not our fault, Mary. She's an 'eadstrong lass, we know that. And I reckon she's well able to look after 'erself."

"But George, she is only a girl and on her own. We must go after her. We can't wait for the Constable and his men to get here from the village. We just *can't!*"

She stared at him, suddenly wondering if his dislike of the Earl in his world of wealth and privilege would stop him from helping the young American girl.

George frowned, then he pulled her close and gave her a hug. He hated to see his sweetheart looking so upset.

"Now, Mary, you know me better than that. The Earl and me come from different walks of life, that's true, but 'e's a true Yorkshireman, the same as me, and no rotten criminal is going to 'old 'im to ransom while I have breath in my body!"

"Then what shall we do?"

George looked grim.

"I reckon you're right – we must go after them! And fast."

*

Half a mile away from the castle, Jasmina was bent double across the pony's mane, her teeth chattering in the cold as the snow blew into her face, settling thickly on her head, darkening her blonde curls to clinging amber strands.

The hoof prints of the horses in the snow ahead of her were rapidly vanishing and she urged the pony into a faster walk.

She realised that she must keep the marks in sight, otherwise the Earl could vanish into the wild moorlands surrounding Somerton. And perhaps never be seen again!

She felt they were making their way round the lake.

Occasionally when the wind blew the snow to one side, she caught a glimpse of the sullen ice to her left.

'Oh, Richard, I would love to skate on the lake with you again. But together, not arguing about the rights and wrongs of my behaviour!'

Suddenly the marks forked – the way to the left continued round the lake, the right-hand track led up into the hills.

Jasmina could make out that the tracks led towards the lake, but the snow was falling so fast now that even her pony's hoof prints would be covered up within minutes.

She must let the rescue party know which way to go, so quickly she pulled the pink velvet ribbon from her hair and, leaning over, tied it to a branch.

Then she urged George's pony onwards, along the kidnappers' trail.

Glancing back once, she could see the pink ribbon for a few seconds, waving valiantly in the wind and then it was lost to view.

With a sob she turned back once more.

Was it really only just a few hours ago that she had walked down the castle's stairs to dine alone with the Earl, feeling so happy and pretty in her dark pink velvet dress?

She felt so cold now that she could hardly feel her hands and feet.

Then, suddenly, just as she thought she could ride no further, she saw a light ahead!

Surely, it must be the kidnappers. No one else was likely to be abroad on such a wild night.

She slowed the pony and peered cautiously through the falling snow.

There seemed to be a large wooden building at the edge of the water and it was from a window that the light was shining dimly through the blizzard.

Jasmina realised it must be the lake's boatshed, a

place used to store not only boats but oars, sails and fishing equipment.

There was one just like it on the Duke of Harley's lake on the other side of the valley.

'They have taken Richard there! Perhaps they have decided to shelter in the boatshed until dawn before they make their escape."

Wincing at the stiffness in her limbs, Jasmina slid off the pony's back, tied him to a tree and crept forward.

The snowstorm had stopped by now and the air felt clear and frosty.

She knew deep in her very being that she was close to Richard.

She could sense him.

She believed that her heart would never lie to her and that whenever they were near to each other, she would always know.

She eased her way carefully along the side of the boatshed until she reached the window and peered in.

Jasmina could see the three men!

Two of them were sitting under the wooden canopy by the lakeside with blankets draped across their shoulders, tearing chunks of meat off a roast chicken.

There were several bottles of beer in front of them and they were laughing loudly.

The third man – the bearded one Jasmina now knew had stolen Lightning – was sitting silently a little apart, just inside the opening of the boatshed, wrapped in his cloak, sipping from a silver brandy flask.

But she could not see Richard! What had they done with him?

Had they hurt the man she loved so much?

Then she noticed that at the very back of the shed, a pair of wide wooden doors stood open to the weather.

There on the muddy ground, half sitting, half lying, his hands bound behind his back, was Richard, the Earl of Somerton!

Jasmina stared in horror.

There was blood on his forehead and dark bruises marked his face. Was he alive?

Then she saw a movement and heard a low groan.

Gasping with relief, Jasmina hurried to the doorway and bending down she slid inside, hidden from the men's gaze by a large motorboat that was raised up on a wooden frame ready for its winter overhaul.

"Richard! My Lord!" she whispered.

For a moment there was no reply, but then the dark head moved slightly.

"Richard! Oh, please answer me."

"*Jasmina?*"

His voice was heavy with amazement and disbelief.

"Oh, you are alive. Oh, thank you, God. I was so scared."

"My dear girl, have you taken leave of your senses? What are you doing here?"

The Earl glanced along the boat shed to where the three men were sitting in the shelter of the far end.

Wincing with pain from his tightly bound wrists, he rolled over so that his back was resting against the wooden frame where Jasmina was crouching.

"I followed you, Richard."

The Earl closed his eyes for a second. He could not believe what he was hearing.

Surely this was the bravest, most wonderful girl in the whole world.

115

But he had to tell her,

"That is the maddest, craziest, most ridiculous – "

"Hush! They will hear you! It might be mad, but it certainly is not ridiculous. I have sent the servants for help from the village. The Constable will surely find us soon."

"Listen, Jasmina – "

"Richard, push your hands backwards a little and I will try to free you. I cannot come any closer or they will see me."

"No, dear girl. You must not put yourself into any more danger. Listen, Jasmina – "

She felt her blood race at the warm feelings in his voice.

"Can you see the tall bearded man?"

"Yes," Jasmina whispered.

"Does he have a black briefcase near to him?"

Jasmina craned forward, then squeaked as her foot slipped and a piece of loose metal crashed to the floor.

The men looked up, but the Earl rolled on his side, groaning, to hide the noise and they relaxed again.

"Keep quiet, your Lordship," one of them sneered. "Or I'll come over there and make you silent for ever!"

"Yes, I can see it," Jasmina murmured as the men turned to their meal. "He has put it on a box next to him."

The Earl moaned, but this time it was not because of the pain in his head where he had been hit.

It was appalling to think that the documents inside that briefcase were headed for a foreign power.

It could mean war.

"Is it the briefcase they came for?" asked Jasmina.

She could just about reach the Earl's wrists and her fingers were pulling helplessly at the tight knots.

"Yes, they don't want *me* at all. The kidnapping is a smokescreen. They think people will wait for a ransom demand, not realising that their target has always been the papers in my briefcase. There are notes, ideas and plans of an extremely sensitive nature and I cannot begin to tell you how important they are to the future of Europe."

"But, Richard, how do they hope to get them out of the valley? The pass is still closed and all this fresh snow will make it doubly difficult to travel."

"Yes, that is what I thought at first, then I realised there is a river that runs from the lake. It is rarely frozen. I think they must have a boat moored nearby and will use it to escape."

"What shall I do?" sighed Jasmina.

In utter despair, she tugged fiercely at the knots, but without a knife, she did not think she would ever free him.

The Earl glanced over to where she was crouching in the dark, his brown eyes full of alarm.

"Nothing at all!" he hissed. "Listen, Jasmina, you must not stay here and place yourself in any more danger. If, as you say, you have already raised the alarm, then hopefully I will be found very soon.

"Return to the castle and tell everyone where I am. Then I will at least know you are safe. And that means so much to me."

Jasmina's heart sang at his words, but she realised at once that she could not leave him.

"Richard, if these documents are really as important as you say, then my safety cannot be a consideration."

The Earl groaned under his breath.

"Dear girl, your safety means the world to me. If only – "

Jasmina reached out her hand and touched his wrist just above where the ropes cut cruelly into his skin.

"Richard, you will never know how I have longed and dreamed to hear those words, but our feelings must not be allowed to interfere with what is right. Evil must never win. Now, tell me what to do."

"Jasmina!"

"Listen, Richard, I know you think women should be protected from all the hazards of this modern world, but surely you must see that this is one of those desperate times when you will have to put that wonderful sentiment aside."

The Earl was silent for several seconds. He knew she was right, but how could he ask the woman he loved to put her life in danger?

"That briefcase must *never* be allowed to leave the country," he muttered, his voice hoarse with anguish.

Jasmina did not hesitate.

There was no time for fond farewells or last minute speeches.

The man she loved had told her what needed to be done and she was determined to do it.

She allowed her fingers to rest for another moment on his bound hands and then she crawled away out into the snowy countryside.

*

Only a mile away, Mary and George were skating slowly along the lake, hand in hand, straining their eyes for any sight of Jasmina on the path that ran along the bank.

The snow had just stopped and the clouds had given way to a brilliant and starry sky with a full moon throwing a silvery light over the white fields and moors.

George had decided the snow was far too deep for them to try and follow the American girl on foot.

Mary had found him a pair of the Earl's skates and it had taken only minutes for the two of them to be out on the ice.

"Miss Winfield must have followed them along the track," said George. "If we keep it in sight, we should see 'er eventually."

"I can't believe she's riding your old pony!" Mary grunted.

They had just been about to set off from the castle when a young groom had run round from the stables with the news that Miss Winfield had taken George's pony and gone off into the night and what should he do?

George grasped Mary's hand tightly as their skates juddered over rough ice.

"She's a real brave lass and no mistake," he agreed. "But she'll be no match for those ruffians even if she does catch up with them."

"Oh, George, what on earth will happen if the Earl is killed? Who will inherit the castle? Where would I go?"

"Now Mary, my sweetheart, stop worrying and just concentrate on finding the two of them alive and well."

"George – look – we're about level to where the path branches. They might have headed up into the hills."

The young farmer swerved to a halt.

"You're right! Stay there while I check it out."

Before she could reply, he had left her side and was scrambling heavily up the bank.

It seemed like an age, but was only seconds before he appeared again through the line of willow trees, waving something in his hand.

"It's a ribbon, Mary. Pink one. Would that belong to Miss Winfield?"

"Yes!" cried Mary in excitement and relief. "She was wearing it in her hair."

"Clever lass has marked the lake path for us. They

haven't gone up into the hills. And I reckon I know where they're 'eaded!"

He slid back down the bank and swooped towards her. Mary reached out and he swung her round in his arms and gave her a rough kiss.

"The boatshed! It's the only place they could rest and shelter this side of the lake. I'll bet you a year's wages that's where they've taken 'is Lordship."

Mary gazed back along the long length of the lake.

The ice glistened silver in the moonlight and in the far distance, she could see the flicker of flares.

Torchlight!

At last the village had been roused and help was on its way.

But would it be in time?

CHAPTER NINE

With her heart thumping wildly, Jasmina now crept slowly around the boat shed, her footsteps muffled in the thick soft snow.

The night was inky dark. The earlier starry sky had vanished as large black clouds swept in across the moors, blanketing the moon and casting everything into gloom.

But luckily the freshly fallen snow gave off plenty of reflected light even in the dark shadowy areas.

She did not know how she had found the courage to leave Richard behind, still bound, a captive of the men who conspired to steal his valuable Government documents.

All she knew was that the agony on the Earl's face had not been caused by his own pain and imprisonment.

Nor did she truly believe that it was putting her life in jeopardy that worried him so much.

No, it was the result of fear of what could happen if those papers were lost and sold to some foreign power.

'Well, they will not leave this country if I can help it!' Jasmina muttered.

'But, oh, dear Heaven, please look after Richard! *Because I love him so much*!'

She paused, wishing she could feel her fingers and toes, which seemed to be frozen solid.

Her love for the Earl was so new and exciting that she wished she had time to sit quietly and savour the thrill that rushed through her at the very sound of his name.

But she could not.

She was on a vital mission and knew she must push everything else to the back of her mind or else that mission would fail.

She now reached the corner of the boatshed and she knew the kidnappers were sheltering just inside, sitting on the wooden jetty surrounding the deep inlet that ran from the lake into the shed.

In the summer she imagined this channel was used to launch the Earl's boat for fishing expeditions and picnics out onto the lake, although Jasmina did not imagine there had been any since his wife died.

She knelt in the snow, glad of the soft leather riding trousers that protected her legs from the cold and listened carefully.

She could hear two of the villains talking away, but could not understand them. Whatever language they were using, it was not one she knew.

She remembered that when she had first seen inside the boatshed, those two had been sitting furthest away from this corner of the building.

The leader of the gang, the bearded one, had been sitting with his back to the wall, sheltering from the wind coming off the lake.

Suddenly he must have stood up, because Jasmina could hear him giving what sounded like brisk orders.

Carefully she peered through the crack between the door and the building.

The two men were grumbling away to each other, but obviously getting ready to move off.

As Jasmina watched, the bearded man strode to the back of the boatshed and she could overhear him taunting Richard and the calm measured sound of his response.

But – and she drew a deep breath – there, lying on the muddy ground was the black briefcase!

He had left it there, so determined was he to make the Earl's life a misery that he had quite forgotten the spoils of his robbery.

This was her chance – probably the only chance she would have.

Jasmina hesitated, but only for a second.

Before she could think of her own safety, she had darted around the edge of the door, snatched the briefcase and turning, fled out across the icy lake.

Inside the bearded foreigner swore viciously as he saw what was happening.

He began to start after Jasmina and just then, the Earl shot out his leg and tripped him up.

He stumbled and fell, cursing, shouting in a foreign language to his two assistants, who looked bewildered by the sudden turn of events and lumbered across the shed to help him, ignoring his shouted orders to follow the girl.

"Oh, Jasmina, run, run! Oh, sweet Heaven, protect my girl," the Earl moaned and struggled to untie his wrists.

There were a few moments of confusion before the men vanished in pursuit of Jasmina and for a second all was silent.

Then suddenly there was a soft movement behind him and a voice called,

"My Lord!"

The Earl turned his head in amazement.

"George Radford! By all that's – ! Quickly, man, untie me. We must go after Miss Winfield. She only has a short start on those ruffians and I fear they will kill her if they catch her."

There was a glint of a blade and George's knife was cutting through the rope.

As he watched the strands giving way, the young farmer laughed to himself.

One quick turn of the blade and the Earl would be dead and no one would ever know who had done it.

George would swear he was dead when he found him.

His farm would be safe because George knew in his heart that the Earl would never give up trying until he had prised it away from the Radford family.

But the wayward thought was just that.

As George had said to Mary, the Earl might be his enemy, but he was an Englishman first and foremost and no foreigner was going to kidnap him while he had any say in the matter.

With a deep groan, the Earl pulled his hands apart, wincing at the ache in his strained arm muscles.

"I thank you very much, Radford. From the bottom of my heart. You had no need to come to my assistance. You are a good man."

Not stopping to pull the rope ends from his wrists, he raced out of the boatshed to desperately gaze across the icy lake, expecting to see Jasmina's fleeing figure with the three men closing in on her.

But the lake lay empty and still before him.

"Where have they gone?" he moaned.

George was at his side, his breath showing in little white clouds in the freezing air.

"The ice perhaps – it cracked – " he murmured, his voice full of dismay.

The Earl shook his head.

"No, thank God. I think not. It is too thick by now to give way, even with four people on it."

"Help is on its way, my Lord. Look – you can see lights flashin' on the far side of the lake. They are torches carried by men from the village. I left Mary back a ways to meet them when they cross the ice to show them where you are. I had guessed that they had you imprisoned in the boatshed."

The Earl nodded, his head whirling.

Yes, the brave men from the village, like George Radford were coming to his aid, as he knew they always would in a real emergency.

But would they be too late to save the life of the woman he loved?

And where was she?

How could she have disappeared so swiftly?

What on earth could have happened to Jasmina and the dastardly kidnappers?

*

As she fled out onto the ice, Jasmina had formed no clear idea of where to go or what to do.

All she knew was that the briefcase must be saved from the Earl's enemies.

Then a sudden thought shot through her brain.

It was not the briefcase that was important – it was the important papers it held!

As she slid and stumbled across the frozen surface, she could hear the sounds of pursuit.

She sharply snapped open the clasp of the briefcase, thanking Heaven that Richard had forgotten to lock it and pulled out a large sheaf of papers, all tied together with red ribbon.

Next she flung the briefcase as far away from her as she could and, pushing the papers firmly inside her jacket, she turned and slid over the ice towards the castle bank.

How long would it take for her pursuers to discover they did not possess their spoils any more?

Hopefully enough time for her to find somewhere to hide the papers.

Or should she destroy them?

Were they replaceable?

The Earl had not said.

'Oh, why did you not ask him, you silly stupid girl! Instead of fussing about what he might think of you,' she moaned as she clambered through the snow, up the bank to the path that ran round the lake.

As she looked back, the moon came out briefly and she could make out three figures quite plainly, bent over what she was sure was the briefcase lying on the ice.

Jasmina gazed around her.

Where could she go?

Where could she possibly hide so she could not be discovered and forced to hand over these vital documents that Richard had been prepared to die to protect?

"Miss Winfield!"

Jasmina almost leapt out of her skin.

"Mary! Oh, my goodness, Mary, how wonderful to see you. But what are you doing here? You'll be caught. Look at those men out on the lake. They are the ones who kidnapped the Earl."

Mary nodded.

"Help is well on its way. And George has gone to release his Lordship. George thought he would be in the old boatshed. Did they demand a ransom? Was that why they grabbed him? I have heard it's a very popular crime nowadays."

Jasmina shook her head.

"No, it was not the Earl they were after. It is these documents!"

And she pressed her hand against the package she had safely hidden under her jacket.

Mary stared in disbelief.

How could some boring old papers be worth all this trouble? It did not make any sense to her.

"Quick, Mary, they've seen us!" gasped Jasmina, as she saw the men look across the ice towards them.

"George's pony is right here, miss!" urged Mary, as they stumbled through the willow trees to where Jasmina had tethered him. "You can ride the papers to safety."

Jasmina swung herself onto the broad grey back.

"I'll not go without you, Mary."

She leant down and holding her arm, Mary vaulted onto the pony behind her, tucking up her long black skirt over her black stockings.

Mary was a country girl and riding bareback held no qualms for her.

However, she could only marvel to herself that this young American lady in leather riding trousers that had seemed so shocking when first seen was just as much at home riding without a saddle as she was.

Jasmina urged the pony forward along the path.

The snow was still deep and he plodded slowly and carefully along, no matter how much she tried to make him go faster.

Mary gazed behind her.

A few hundred yards away, she could see the men

floundering through the deep snow, but they were gaining ground.

She bit her lip.

She realised that her extra weight was the problem. George's poor old pony could not cope with two riders at the same time.

Suddenly she had made up her mind and slid to the ground.

"*Mary*!"

"Don't stop, madam! Keep going. I'll try and lead them away from you."

Jasmina felt her heart breaking at Mary's bravery, but knew she had no choice.

She urged the pony forward and without the extra load, he quickened his pace, heading for the castle and the comfort of the warm stables.

*

As the Earl and George gazed around for signs of Jasmina and her pursuers, a sudden commotion broke out a little way down the lakeside.

A figure shot out from the shelter of the tall willow trees and slid across the ice.

Within a few seconds, two burly men followed her, slipping and sliding, but closing in fast.

"That's my Mary!" cried George and flung himself forward out of the boatshed.

The Earl hesitated. He could see the torches of the villagers coming across the lake from the other bank.

They would soon reach Mary and the villains and George was more than capable of taking on two men at once to protect his sweetheart.

But yet there was no sign of Jasmina or the bearded foreigner.

In a brief flash he knew what had happened. Those brave wonderful girls had separated in order to throw their pursuers off the track.

And it had half worked.

The two men who, even now, were being subdued by George and an angry group of villagers, had followed Mary.

But the leader of the gang had obviously not been so easily distracted from his goal.

He must have stayed on Jasmina's trail.

The Earl was certain that she would not have parted with the papers. They were still in danger of being wrested back and so Jasmina's life was still at risk.

Grimly he forced his way back to the path, his heart bursting with fear for the beautiful outspoken creature with tumbling yellow curls and bright sapphire blue eyes, who had come to mean so much to him in such a short while.

The tracks there were quite plain.

The deep even hoof prints of a heavily laden pony and, over the top of them, the marks of a horse that was shying and skittering and all the time being forced along the track towards Somerton Castle.

*

Jasmina felt herself swaying violently as the sturdy pony plodded into the castle grounds.

She was so very tired and cold she could not think clearly.

All she really wanted to do was to crawl into her bed and sleep for a month.

But she knew that was a luxury that was denied her at the moment.

Not while she was still responsible for the secret papers and could help Richard, the man she loved so much.

She slid off the pony with a groan as he reached the main steps, certain he would find his own way round to the stables.

Glancing over her shoulder, she thought she could just hear the chink of a bit and the creak of a saddle, but the moon had vanished again and the darkness of the castle cast a deep shadow over the pathway.

Running up the steps, she hammered loudly on the door, hoping and praying that one of the footmen would answer.

But to her horror it just swung open under her fists and she stepped into the dark cavernous hall. There was only one small oil lamp burning on a side table, throwing out a tiny circle of light

"Hallo there!" she called, but her voice echoed off the great stone walls and there was no reply.

The suits of armour and ranks of swords and spears glinted in the weak light and far above her head, the wind whistled through an open window.

Jasmina could not understand why no one came to answer her call and then the realisation struck home.

Of course, all the servants would be out searching for the kidnapped Earl!

The castle, which did not boast a large staff because of its Master's solitary existence, was completely empty.

She was about to pick up the oil lamp and head for the kitchen, when she heard sounds on the steps outside.

There was no time for the lamp.

She ran across the darkened hall towards the stairs that vanished up into the blackness above.

She knew that whoever was following her was not a friend and she also knew that she had never been so close to death before.

'Oh, Richard, if only you were here with me,' she whispered. 'I am so scared. *So alone.*'

Gasping for breath and shivering with the cold, she reached the top landing and stared around in desperation.

Where on earth could she hide these vital papers where they would not easily be found?

"It's no good you running any longer, dear lady," came a smooth and accented voice from the hall below. "There is nowhere in this castle where you will be safe from me."

"What do you want?" she shouted back defiantly.

"You know perfectly well what I am wanting, dear madam. Just throw down the papers you are safe-guarding and I will leave and no one will get hurt."

"*Never!* They belong to Lord Somerton and I shall never give them to you!"

"And where is your precious Earl at this moment, may I ask? Is he rushing wildly to your aid? No, indeed! He is my prisoner, Miss Winfield. He is quite unable to help you!"

Jasmina backed her way along the dark corridor that stretched between two of the castle turrets.

The bearded man was now at the top of the stairs, walking slowly but inexorably towards her. His voice was smooth as silk, but a silk that covered a wicked blade.

"Why are you fighting against me, Miss Winfield? You are not an English lady, you hold no allegiance to the Government of this country.

"Why, it is not so many years ago that America fought the British for their independence. So why not just hand over all the documents and then you can go home and forget about this unhappy event."

She backed further away from him towards the end

of the corridor, stumbling in the dark over some broken wood that lay on the floor.

She had no idea of her exact whereabouts and the castle seemed so very big and empty.

The man came even closer, his dark eyes glittering.

"You just cannot win, Miss Winfield," he snarled in his strange accent. "Now hand over the documents to me at once!"

Jasmina glanced around.

There was a small door behind her and she tried to open it, but it was jammed tight and her hands were too cold to force it open.

So now there was nowhere left to run.

She turned and raised her head in proud defiance as the man stepped in front of her.

She was from the United States of America and her people never gave in to tyrants.

"No never! You will have to take them from me," she shouted out at him.

The man sounded angry and puzzled.

"Why are you doing this? You are putting your life in danger – for why? What can this Earl of Somerton be to you?"

Jasmina felt a thrill run through her.

She was now about to die, but at least she would die proclaiming her deepest feelings for the man she loved so much.

"To me he is the dearest man in all the world," she retorted firmly, the passion in her voice making even the kidnapper hesitate.

"I would do anything in my power to help him. He is such a wonderful man, but to me he is not just the Earl of

Somerton, marvellous as his ancient title is. He is simply Richard – the man I love with all my heart and all my soul.

"And if I am about to die, then I will make my way to God above knowing that I have experienced the greatest happiness any woman could find – loving a good man."

She paused, thinking she had just heard a noise in the hall below, placed a hand on the railings and glanced down.

"*Richard*!"

"Jasmina, my love!"

The Earl raced across the hall from the front door.

"Don't you dare touch her, you fiend. Let her go!"

But he was too late.

The foreigner darted forward as Jasmina turned and clutched at her with violent hands.

But she managed to pull the papers from inside her jacket and with the last ounce of her strength, she hurled them over the railings into the hall beneath.

Jasmina heard the man curse at her viciously, heard herself call out Richard's name once more, then everything became a blur.

She was aware of something small and white flying out of an adjacent door and flinging itself into the melee, of struggling to escape the man's clutches, falling against the railings and the terrible cracking noise they made as they gave way.

In the dark she managed to pull herself away from the man and fought to keep her balance as he tripped, lost his balance and vanished without a sound, hurtling to his doom on the stone floor below.

Then she was falling too!

She heard the Earl shout out in terror.

Her fingers somehow managed to catch the edge of the floorboards and she hung there swinging, looking up into the horrified face of dear little Florence, whose white cotton nightgown had been the flying shape she had seen erupt from the door that she realised led to the servants' quarters.

"Madam! Madam! Take my hand, quickly."

Jasmina gasped and looked up at the hand held out to her. It was roughened and reddened by housework and very small.

She knew in an instant that if she took it, Florence would not be strong enough to pull her up.

No, she would only drag her over the edge and they would both plummet to the stone floor beneath them.

"No – listen, Florence, stand back from the edge! It isn't safe."

She realised that she could not hold on, but before she could even send out her last prayer, suddenly Florence was whisked away and the face of the Earl appeared in the gap caused by the broken railings.

"Jasmina, my dearest."

"Richard!"

"Listen, sweetheart. I can pull you up, but when I take hold of your arm, you must let go of the floorboards, otherwise I cannot do it."

Jasmina glanced up into the dark eyes she loved so much.

She could feel her feet kicking in the open space and recognised that her frozen fingers would not be able to grip the wooden edge for much longer.

"Do you trust me, Jasmina?" urged the Earl, lying flat on the ground and reaching down with both hands.

"With all my heart and soul!"

His fingers closed round the soft flesh of her arms where the jacket sleeves had fallen back.

"Now! Let go!"

For a long second Jasmina could not move.

The Earl's dark and passionate gaze met the blazing love in her blue eyes.

What she saw in his look made her heart sing with joy and, without another moment's hesitation, she let go of the wooden edge and hung, suspended for a split second from his grasp until, with all the strength in his being, he pulled her slowly but surely to safety.

CHAPTER TEN

An hour later Somerton Castle was in uproar with a constant line of people arriving and departing.

A roaring fire was blazing in the drawing room and Mrs. Rush was bustling around the kitchen, issuing orders in all directions, providing hot drinks, soup, beer and huge portions of cake and pie to the chattering staff and those villagers who had braved the frozen lake to search for the kidnapped Earl.

Jasmina had been rushed into a hot bath by one of the maids. She had not had any chance to see what was happening in the Great Hall or speak to the Earl after he had pulled her to safety.

Dressed in a heavy velvet wrap, she braided her hair into one thick golden plait that hung down her back and made her look incredibly young.

She made her way down the back stairs as the local Constable and his men were still busy in the Great Hall.

With a weary sigh, she sank deep into a low chair in front of the fire.

She realised from a faint light glimmering through a gap in the curtains that it must be almost dawn, but she could not go to bed until she had seen the Earl.

The door opened and the Earl entered, his hair still wet from his bath.

He was wearing a white shirt, open at the neck, and an old pair of trousers.

Swiftly he ran across the room, caught Jasmina's hands in his and drew her to her feet.

Without saying a word, he dropped a kiss on each finger.

"You are safe!" he sighed at last with a choke.

Jasmina smiled up at him, her blue eyes shining in the firelight.

"Safe and sound, my Lord."

"Richard! We agreed on that and after all we have shared, I could never call you Miss Winfield again!"

A little shudder ran through her as the memory of hanging over the edge of the gallery surged back into her mind.

"That man – ?" she began.

He took hold of her shoulders and looked intently into her face.

"Listen, Jasmina, he is dead. They have taken him away and the other two criminals have been arrested. They cannot hurt anyone again."

"He would have killed me to get the papers and – oh, Richard – what about Florence? She was so brave!"

The Earl smiled at her tenderly. It was just so like his wonderful girl to think of a lowly maid before herself.

"Florence is, I am reliably told, safely tucked up in bed once again. She had apparently been given a tot of brandy in hot milk earlier because her leg was painful. So she was fast asleep and missed all the excitement when I was taken away. When she woke, she crept down the back stairs and realised that you were in grave danger."

Jasmina smiled tremulously, remembering the way the small figure in a long white nightgown had flung itself at the bearded stranger.

"I must find a way of repaying her for her bravery. She did not need to put herself in such danger. I will think of a fitting reward for her courage."

"Talking of courage," said the Earl, "I cannot begin to thank you for what you have done tonight, both for me and for England," playing with the end of the thick braid that lay across her shoulder.

"I do not any need thanks! I was determined to find you and help as best I could. Everyone played their part."

The Earl tilted her face up to his so he could gaze into the depth of the blue eyes he loved so much.

"If anything had happened to you, Jasmina – if you should have been killed or injured, then I would not have wanted to have gone on living myself!"

"Richard – "

"No, listen to me, sweetheart. My feelings for you have grown deeper and deeper as the days have passed. Jasmina, please, please tell me that you don't think me a completely hopeless case and that you have some small tenderness towards me besides that of a good guest for her host?"

Jasmina reached up to push the dark unruly hair off his forehead.

"Richard! You have had my heart for many a day now. Surely you know that?"

With a little gasp, he bent his head and kissed her tenderly and Jasmina felt herself fly up to Heaven with the sheer joy of his kiss.

Then, suddenly, there was a knock at the door and the Earl cursed under his breath.

Henry appeared, announcing that the Constable was still in the hall, wishing to speak to the Earl.

"I will come down in a moment," he snapped.

"He is most insistent, my Lord," Henry responded apologetically. "He has the other two villains in custody and now needs your instructions as to how to proceed."

The Earl sighed and smiled down at Jasmina who had sunk back into her chair.

"My night's work is not over, you see. Forgive me. I must go. We will talk again in the morning when we have both had a good sleep! Things should be more settled by then."

And with a brief nod he was gone.

*

When Jasmina woke up, hours later, she was warm and cosy under her soft blankets and fine silk sheets.

She yawned and stretched luxuriously.

She had been having the most fabulous dream – she had been dancing with the Earl, his arms around her, and they were wonderfully, wonderfully happy!

The light streaming through the curtains was bright and sunny.

"Goodness, how late is it?" she exclaimed and as if in answer to her question, there was a knock at the door and Mary came in.

"Mary! How good to see you. Are you all right? Not injured in any way?"

The housekeeper smiled gravely at her.

"Thank you, I am in good health, madam. Just so relieved that all has ended well and look, one of the village children found this package in the woods and brought it up to the castle. I do believe it is your passport and travel documents, madam!"

"Oh, that is good news indeed."

Jasmina threw back the bedclothes and, pulling on her robe, hurried to the window.

"Why, it must now be the afternoon," she declared. "You should not have let me sleep so long."

"I am afraid we are all at sixes and sevens today, Miss Winfield. As you can see, a thaw set in a couple of hours ago. The ice is already thinning on the lake."

"I must dress at once," said Jasmina. "I do hope the Earl has not waited to have a meal with me."

Mary stopped tidying the room and frowned.

"Oh, the Earl is not at Somerton at the moment."

Jasmina stared at her.

"Not at Somerton?"

"Why, no. The telephone lines were repaired this morning and there was an urgent call from London for him. He left immediately."

Jasmina tried not to let her disappointment show.

She sank down in front of the dressing table mirror and began to unbraid her hair, her fingers running over the locks that the Earl had touched so tenderly the night before.

"To London?"

Mary nodded, worried that all the life and joy had vanished from Jasmina's face.

"Yes. Word came that the way over the moors to Debbingford is passable. He left as soon as he could pack. I believe those documents that those dreadful men were so keen to steal had to be in London immediately."

"Of course. But he will return – when?"

The housekeeper hesitated.

"Why, I don't know, madam, but I am sure he will not stay in the City a moment longer than he has to."

"Did he give no indication of when he would return or leave a note for me?"

Mary heard the strained, wistful tone in her voice, but reluctantly had to say,

"No, madam. There was no note."

Mary hesitated at the doorway. Along with the rest of the staff and her own sweetheart, George Radford, she was convinced that the Earl had strong feelings for Jasmina Winfield.

He had become a different man since the American girl's arrival at Somerton.

Gone was the gloomy and despondent air that had surrounded him since the death of his wife.

Everyone in the castle had noted the change in him and there was no one who was not pleased and delighted.

So were they engaged? Surely an announcement would have been made if they were.

"Is there anything else, madam?"

Jasmina fought back her tears.

"No, thank you, Mary. I shall be down directly, as soon as I have dressed."

When she had left the room, Jasmina stared at her reflection in the mirror.

What a fool she was!

What had she been thinking!

That the Earl of Somerton, an English aristocrat of ancient lineage, who could marry into the highest circles of Society, would propose marriage to a girl he had just met?

How ridiculous!

Everything he had said to her the night before had probably been said in the heat of the moment, in relief at his rescue and that she had helped save his precious papers.

'I accept that he himself had to carry the documents to London, but surely he would never have left without a word to me if his feelings had been as strong as my own?' she whispered to herself, wiping the tears from her cheeks with fingers that shook with emotion.

No, all she could imagine was that in the cold light of day, he had used the excuse of a long journey, far away from Somerton, to bring to an end the difficult relationship he could see he had brought about.

'No note! Nothing at all! Well, that does tell me everything,' Jasmina thought grimly and dressed as fast as she could.

Mary was attempting to bring some sort of order to the Great Hall as she ran down the stairs.

Maids and footmen were clearing away the remains of the broken railings and washing and scrubbing the grey flagstones.

Mary looked up in surprise.

It had only seemed minutes since she had spoken to Miss Winfield and here she was, dressed, ready to –

"You are going riding, madam?" she asked her in astonishment, taking in the muddy leather trousers she had been wearing the day before.

"Indeed, Mary. I imagine my horse, Lightning, has been stabled overnight at the castle. That – " she glanced at the place where the bearded kidnapper had fallen – "man was riding him, I know he was."

"Yes, George found your horse tethered outside and one of the young grooms took care of him. But, Miss Winfield, where are you going now?"

Jasmina turned a bright forced smile on her.

"Why, to stay with my relations at the Parsonage in Debbingford, of course. It will soon be Christmas and they are expecting me to stay with them for the festivities. I will be grateful if you would arrange for my heavy luggage to be sent over by carrier immediately. I shall take just my small travel bag with me."

"But his Lordship may be back soon – "

Jasmina held out a hand in an abrupt gesture.

"I am sure he will be very busy in London and, as you can see, I cannot remain here at the castle, Mary. Why should I? I have always been an uninvited guest here and Richard – the Earl – has not asked me to stay!"

Mary swallowed her reply as Jasmina turned away, fearing she had revealed too much.

She looked in horror at the bright tears brimming in the girl's big blue eyes.

This was all wrong, but there was nothing she could say to make it better.

And so a small group gathered on the steps of the castle to wave goodbye to Jasmina as she rode away, only accompanied by a young groom.

Mary had insisted she did not travel through the pass to the next valley on her own.

Although the snow had partially melted, the going was still bad and Mary knew it was more than her job was worth to allow a visitor to the castle to travel without an escort and, reluctantly, Jasmina had agreed.

George Radford joined Mary on the steps. He had come to the castle to fetch his little pony, the one that had played such an important part in the Earl's rescue.

He gazed up at the sky. The blue of the afternoon had gone and it was a sullen grey again.

"Bad weather is on its way again, Mary, my love. These old moors haven't given us much respite after all."

She nodded, waving until the two horses were out of sight.

"I reckon Miss Winfield will just have time to get across to Debbingford before the snow returns! Oh, if only it had snowed again last night, the Earl would have been forced to stay at the castle and they may well have sorted out everything today."

George ruffled his dark red hair.

"Gentry don't always think the same way as us."

Mary sighed.

"Then the gentry are stupid! Those two are made for each other. Anyone can see that."

George took her hand between his.

"You look real upset, sweetheart. There's nothin' you can do." He bent his head and gave her a quick kiss. "Now, how about askin' Ma Rush to make me a nice meat pasty before I head back to the farm?"

Mary bit her lip.

She realised that, as much as she loved George, the chance of them ever getting married was slim.

He was determined never to sell his rundown farm to the Earl and without that money, they would never have enough to set up home together.

For some reason Mary had been thrilled to think of a love story coming to a happy ending in front of her and now – well, she reckoned Miss Winfield was as unhappy as she was herself.

With tears in her eyes, she turned away, back into the castle.

George followed her, frowning. He was a hard-headed farmer, a man of few words, unused to showing his emotions or even admitting to having many tender feelings.

But he did love Mary and hated to see her so upset. And apparently it was just because the Earl's romance with Miss Winfield seemed to have fallen through!

He paused at the top of the steps to gaze out across the grassy slope towards the lake and on to the distant pass in the hills that led to Debbingford.

Big fat flakes of snow were already falling and if it continued to fall and the weather closed in again, George reckoned that the Earl might find it difficult to return to the castle for some time.

He rubbed his chin thoughtfully.

The Earl was a Lord and an aristocrat, but beneath all that, he was just a man, the same as himself.

Did he understand women any more than he did?

The redheaded farmer had the oddest feeling that the Earl had gone to London believing that his young lady would still be here at the castle when he returned.

Females had flights of fancy that mere men did not. Miss Winfield had rushed away to Debbingford and now his Mary was all of a bother over the situation.

'Well, I don't much care about 'is Lordship and Miss Winfield, but I'm damned if I'll have Mary upset!'

And with a determined look on his face, George made his way back inside the castle.

*

Two days later, the snow that had fallen had frozen over once again.

The pond in the village of Debbingford was frozen solid and the local children had been skating on it in happy excitement, but today they were either in the schoolhouse or helping their parents on their farms.

Jasmina was alone on the pond and her blades cut smoothly through the ice as she circled round.

The cold air stung her eyes and throat and was the excuse she gave herself for the tears that froze on her pink cheeks.

They certainly were not tears of regret for the Earl of Somerton, she told herself crossly. She refused to live a life looking back at what might have been.

She skated round the pond again, slowly this time.

She loved her relatives and the Parson was elderly and a sweet, kind-hearted gentleman, if somewhat absent-minded.

He could muddle up Jasmina with her grandmother, who had been his sister, as apparently they looked very much alike.

The Parsonage was also home to his two daughters, Hope and Faith, spinsters who were both overjoyed to meet their relation from America and did all in their power to spoil her dreadfully.

'Yes, I am having a lovely time here,' Jasmina said to herself. 'And I refuse to think of Richard any more. As soon as Christmas is over, I will be heading back down to London and then across the ocean to America. What a lot I shall have to tell my friends and family there!'

And what a lot she would have to hide from them!

The thought flashed through her like an arrow.

She allowed the memories of her time at Somerton Castle to flood through her mind – she could picture the Earl's dark eyes looking down at her, still feel the warmth of his lips on hers.

Suddenly, Jasmina let out a little scream.

Someone had skated up behind her and was pulling her round, his hand on her arm –

"Miss Winfield! I claim the next dance!"

"*Richard*!"

The name was scarcely past her lips when she was pulled close to him, his arm was around her waist and they were skating, dancing together across the sparkling ice.

Held closely in his arms, they sped round the pond, their blades cutting patterns together, their laughter rising up towards Heaven itself.

Jasmina cast a glance up at him.

The Earl was smiling, all the dark depression had vanished and he looked so young and *so* handsome.

She wished they could dance like this forever.

She felt as though she was in Paradise itself and somehow the brass doors had opened and she had walked through, arm in arm with her beloved man.

But at last their dance came to an end as the pale sun now dipped behind the square Norman Church tower and the temperature began to fall.

The Earl braked to a dead halt in a shower of ice and wrapped his arms tightly around her.

"You ran away from me, Jasmina," he murmured solemnly, "that is why I have come to kidnap you, to take you back to the castle where you belong."

Jasmina stared up into his face, her eyes two blue shining stars.

"I did not run away from you, Richard. I came here because I was scared you did not love me. You left me no word and I could not presume – "

The Earl stopped her words with a kiss.

"I was at fault. Forgive me, darling girl. I thought you realised how I felt, that you would stay at the castle and wait for me to return. It was not until George Radford telephoned me – "

"George telephoned you?"

Richard chuckled at the expression on her face.

"Yes, indeed. It was so unexpected and alarming. He obviously doesn't use a telephone often and thought he had to shout at the top of his voice! I think I could have heard him in London without the use of the telephone!"

"But what did he say?"

"Not a lot, just that Miss Winfield had departed for Debbingford, that it was snowing hard and if I didn't come back to Yorkshire immediately I was a bigger damn fool than he had thought!"

"Richard!"

The Earl laughed.

"It was impertinence of the highest kind, but he will always deserve my undying gratitude. And I know exactly how to reward him.

"But at the moment, he has instructions to find the tallest Christmas tree he can and carry it to the castle. It will need decorating, so will you please come home with me for Christmas, Jasmina? Will your relations allow you to stay there unchaperoned, or do I need to kidnap you for real, because I am never letting you go again!"

Jasmina smiled tenderly, her eyes full of joy.

"You have no need to kidnap me, I shall come most willingly with you. And I am sure one of my cousins will be thrilled to accompany me, if not both of them!"

Richard smoothed back the golden curls that were escaping their bonds and framing her face.

"And will you be my *wife*, Miss Jasmina Winfield? Will you do me the greatest honour any woman can bestow on a man and give me your hand in marriage?"

Jasmina stood on tiptoe and even though she knew she should sound suitably demure and modest, she kissed him, laughing at the surprised expression that crossed his face before he returned her embrace.

"I would love to be your wife, Richard!" she sighed eagerly. "It is my heart's desire above all else."

"And you will not mind giving up your *American independence* to become the Countess of Somerton with all the responsibilities that title brings?"

Jasmina smiled tenderly.

"I believe I shall always keep my independent spirit and I am sure that you would never want to curb it. But I look forward to everything the future holds.

"And most of all, I look forward to sharing our love together in this beautiful country, which I shall delight in making mine. And I know that in time I shall be able to travel with you to Missouri and show you the wonders of my world as well."

"And your parents? What will they say? I must speak to your father. Will he object to you living so far away? Surely they will miss you."

Jasmina sighed.

It was the only small cloud on her horizon.

"Yes, they will miss me. But they are not old, they love to travel and I am sure they will visit here many times.

"St. Louis is often called the Gateway to the West, as it is where the wagon trains all set off, taking settlers out to distant parts of America. Well, this time it will be the gateway back to the Old World."

Richard kissed her again.

"I never thought I could find such happiness. I feel as though I have been locked inside a dark room and only now can I open the door and see the light. You have saved me, Jasmina, saved me from a life spent in dreary darkness and guilt and I will always love you for it.

"Now, let us go and tell your relations our news and plan for our festivities. This will be the happiest and best Christmas the castle has seen for many years!"

*

And it was indeed a wonderful, joy-filled time, full of colour and music and laughter.

The staff told each other that there had never been such a happy Christmas at the castle with branches of holly and greenery in every room and the giant Christmas tree standing in the Great Hall, ablaze with candles.

But Christmas was just a happy memory, the snow and ice vanished and the sky a cloudless spring blue when the most important day of Jasmina's life dawned.

The Earl had been determined to marry in the local Church and not in the great Minster at York.

The fields were full of daffodils and newborn lambs gambolled in the fields as the wedding guests gathered at the old Norman church in Somerton village.

Every pew was packed, the American guests proud and happy to witness such a glorious event of a daughter of the New World marrying a son of the Old.

Jasmina's mother was sitting next to the Duke and Duchess of Harley. The Duchess, of course, held herself completely responsible for the romance.

"After all," she said, with a twinkle in her eye, "if I hadn't left her alone, they might never have met!"

In a pew just behind the aristocratic guests sat the castle staff, resplendent in new clothes.

Mary and George Radford sat on the other side of the Church.

They had been married a fortnight earlier and had been very proud that the guests of honour at their wedding had been the Earl and Miss Winfield.

Mary was no longer the housekeeper at the castle. She was now a farmer's wife, for the Earl had kept his word and repaid George in the way he knew would be best.

The Radford farm was now owned jointly by him

and George and it would stay in both families for ever and whatever the land produced would be shared equally.

Now the Church organ sounded and all eyes turned to the door.

Florence was sitting in the back pew of the Church. Her new spring coat was bright blue with brass buttons that shone in the soft candlelight.

She was with her father and not with the other staff, because Florence was no longer working at the castle!

Mr. and Mrs. Winfield had offered to take her and her father back to America with them when they left! They were going to work for the family in Missouri and travel on a big ship across the world to another country and see all those strange places with strange names like Mississippi!

Florence's reward for her bravery was so exciting she could not stop smiling.

Then, as the Church doors opened, her eyes became wide with wonder.

Jasmina walked slowly past her on her father's arm.

She looked like an angel, the pure white of her lace dress and the long veil that trailed behind her in a wide fan, gleaming in the dusky candlelight.

She was carrying a great sheaf of white lilies and roses, whilst the flowers in her headdress were all wild primroses, picked from the hedgerows around Somerton that very morning.

Richard, the Earl of Somerton, turned, catching his breath as his bride reached his side.

She was all spring in his eyes.

A glorious girl bringing new life and hope to his family.

He reached for her hand as the old and wonderful words rang out, his eyes full of love and adoration.

Jasmina felt as if she was suspended in a floating bubble of joy.

She was marrying Richard, the man she loved so deeply and so much.

Her heart soared and she had never imagined that she could ever feel so happy in all her life.

This was real Love, the love the poets had written about since the beginning of time.

Marrying Richard was the true way to Heaven and although she was far from her home, Jasmina knew that, completely secure in the love they both shared, they would create a wonderful new life together here on Earth.